D1004889

The Librarian

Unhappily Ever After

Eric Hobbs

Eric Hobbs
4026 Highland Springs Drive
Kokomo, IN 46902

Ordering Information: Special discounts are available on quantity purchases by corporations, associations, and others. For details, contact the publisher at the address above.

Kokomo, IN / Eric Hobbs – First Edition

ISBN 9780692743126

Printed in the United States of America

For McKensie,
who probably forgets these books were
always for her

CHAPTER 1

TAYLOR WAS STANDING in the library's main hall, though she had no recollection of why she was there or how she'd arrived. In fact, when she heard a familiar voice call her name, she knew it was only possible in a dream.

"Taylor?" It was a nurturing voice, gentle and warm. "I thought there was something you wanted to show me."

Taylor grinned. She quickly began to scan the room.

The old building was alive with activity. College students stood shoulder-to-shoulder at the card catalogue. Smiling children wormed their way through the musty aisles in search of books. A tall, bearded man appeared from the Archives Room with a long scroll of paper tucked under his arm and beamed like he'd just made a major discovery.

It's not her. You're crazy, Tay. It can't—

Taylor's breath caught in her chest.

"Mom?"

Taylor's mother, Karen, was standing just a few feet away beneath the skylight in the library's domed ceiling.

"Oh my god," Taylor squealed. "Mom!"

Taylor covered the ground between them in an instant and wrapped both arms around her mother's waist.

"Whoa!" Karen said. "Where'd that come from?"

"Where'd that come from?" Taylor's bear hug was nearly enough to squeeze the air from Karen's lungs. "What are you *doing* here?!"

Taylor pulled away just enough so she could look her mom over. Karen's skin was flawless; her hair fell like a waterfall over one shoulder just like Tay's; her smile was ever-present. She looked exactly as Taylor remembered, and yet, there were countless details Taylor had forgotten - like the way she stood with her hands clasped in front of her or the tarnished ring that never left the pinky finger of her left hand. She was perfect. It was like a talented artist had captured Karen on her best day. Even her black dress, a dress which seemed strangely familiar, was gorgeous.

The Astoria Library really *was* a magical place.

A place where dreams came true.

Karen smiled. "It's our mother-daughter date. Remember? But you said we had to come here first. To the library. You said there was something you wanted to show me."

Taylor tried to shake the cobwebs from her head. She didn't remember any of this, but she knew there *was* something she wouldn't let her mom leave without seeing. She offered a tiny hand for Karen to take, and they started across the room together.

"You won't believe it," Taylor whispered. "It's the most amazing thing."

She led Karen to the literature display near a smooth pillar in the center of the room. Both were so caught up in the moment that neither noticed they were now alone in the library. All the people who'd been with them just moments before, we're gone.

Taylor grinned as she looked the exhibit over. All the relics from Oz were in their rightful places, just as she and Wesley had left them. The silver slippers were there, sitting side-by-side near the oil can and the three yellow bricks. Even the magic wand they'd use to access the portal was back in place, lying alongside the thick, leather-bound book on its pedestal.

"Watch," Taylor giggled.

Up on her tiptoes, Taylor leaned over the display's velvet rope and grabbed the wand before Karen had a chance to react.

"What are you doing? You can't just–"

"Wait," Taylor said. "Just wait. You'll see."

She started down one of the library's long aisles, and her mother followed, both heading toward the wooden piece of art that was hanging on–

❖ ❖ ❖

Taylor was standing in the Tin Man's cabin, though she had little recollection of why she was there or how she'd arrived. In fact, her thoughts were so clouded that all she could remember was–

Her heart sank. "Mom? *Mom?*"

She whipped around in a panic, worried her mother might have been left behind. But Karen was there, watching with awe as the last of the portal's light disappeared with a wink.

"I... I..." Karen couldn't believe it. "What just happened? *How did you do that?*"

"C'mon," Taylor said. "You ain't seen nothing yet."

Karen took Taylor's hand once more, shutting her eyes when the room filled with light and–

◆ ◆ ◆

Taylor and Karen were skipping down the yellow brick road with their arms linked; both were singing the same wrong words to a song from a film they'd watched more times than either could remember. When finished, they were laying in the meadow, doubled over with laughter as tears of joy streamed down their cheeks. They had little recollection of why they were there or how they'd arrived, but they were having so much fun that neither really cared.

It was a mother-daughter date.

The best they'd ever had.

Maybe the best anyone would ever have.

Nothing else mattered.

This was how their day progressed, a brilliant flash reliably transporting them from one place to the next, their adventure in Oz a beautiful collage of stolen moments in time...

They toured Emerald City while wearing the oversized spectacles given to them by the Guardian of the Gate. They picnicked beneath the Great Waterfall near the palace of Glinda the Good. They traveled to China Country, where Taylor explained that the land made of fragile glass looked nothing like she'd imagined when reading about it in the *Oz* books.

One flash took them from Oz to the farmlands of Kansas where they hid in the brush and watched as Dorothy was reunited with her aunt. Taylor gave her mother a bitter-sweet look, convinced their own story would have an ending equal to that of Dorothy and Em's.

But eventually daylight waned and their time in Oz came to an end. They started back, following the road of yellow bricks, no flash of light to help them along this time. As they walked, Taylor noticed that the vibrant vista of Oz was slowly beginning to fade as the sun slipped beneath the horizon. It wasn't the natural change one might expect at dusk: that magic hour between day and night. Instead, everything seemed muted, like they were looking at the world through a dirty pane of glass.

And there was more.

Birds circled overhead. Dark thunderclouds mounted in the distance. The wind began to gust.

Taylor quickened her pace. Her mother followed suit.

Taylor pointed down a worn path that cut through the woods. “This way.”

“Are you sure?” Karen asked. “The road goes around.”

“If we go that way we’ll never make it before dark. We'll be fine. You'll see.” There was only a hint of doubt in her voice.

The forest offered shelter from the changing landscape, but this did little to ease their nerves as the tree limbs cast dark, wraith-like shadows across their path. They followed the winding trail until they reached the shortcut’s end where they found a black dog waiting for them.

“Awe!” Taylor exclaimed. They'd met a number of animals during their trip. Most were of the cute and cuddly variety. Standing in shadow, this dog looked to be no different. It actually *did* look like it was waiting for them, as if it were there to escort them the rest of the way home.

"Come here. I won't hurt you, big guy."

Tay stepped toward it, but Karen raised an arm to stop her.

"Wait."

The dog's coat was matted. Its dry skin was stretched tightly across its bones. It turned toward them, and Taylor flinched when she saw it was missing an ear and staring at them with eyes that glowed red.

"That's not a dog. That's–"

"A wolf," Karen finished.

Karen took Taylor's hand. They stepped forward together.

"Easy," Karen whispered.

The wolf snarled. Long strings of drool spilled from the wolf's mouth. Its lip curled, baring two rows of razor-sharp teeth stained yellow and pink.

Karen felt Taylor tense up and squeezed her hand.

"Don't look back."

But Taylor had to look.

While she couldn't see its body, Taylor saw the red-hot eyes of another wolf appear in the darkness behind them. Others came. Then more. Behind them, beside them, everywhere, until eventually they were surrounded by the entire pack.

"One step at a time," Karen said. "We're almost there."

A sound like gravel rattled in the wolf's throat as they walked past. Then, it barked, and the pack charged out of the darkness after them.

"Run!" Karen screamed.

Taylor bolted down the path and out of the woods.

"What's happening?!"

The colors outside the forest were no longer muted. They'd faded completely. Tay felt like they were running through an old, silent film. Everything around them was colored in monochromatic shades of grey. Her movements felt jerky and uncontrolled.

The Tin Man's cabin appeared on the horizon.

"Look," Karen hollered. "We're almost there!"

Never stopping, Taylor quickly glanced back.

The savage pack was closing in. Growling. Barking. Snarling. Red eyes alive with hate. Hundreds of teeth were exposed, ready to do their master's bidding.

Taylor checked the distance that remained between them and the cabin.

Mom's right, she thought. *Almost there! Almost there! Almost—*

Taylor tripped to the ground. Her mother did, too. Both stumbled face first into the grass, neither able to break her fall.

"Get up, girl! Move!"

Taylor tried to right herself, but her foot wouldn't give. She looked back, half expecting to find that her foot was caught under a fallen limb or hooked behind a large rock. Instead, her eyes grew wide with horror when she found the true culprit was the ground beneath her. It had given way like quicksand and swallowed her foot whole.

"Pull!" Karen screamed. *"Pull!"*

Taylor watched Karen yank her foot free and tried to do the same. The earth loosened its grip but kept the sandal she'd been wearing.

"Go!" Karen ordered. "I'm right behind!"

"But, Mom—"

"Go!"

The wolves were almost on them. Taylor took off, but only made it a few steps before her foot broke through the ground's surface again. This time, she pulled free before falling but was now running barefoot through the meadow.

"Don't look back!"

"Are you coming?"

"I'm with you! Go!"

Taylor could hear the hungry mob right on their heels. She tried to push her pace, but every stride seemed to slow her progress. Her feet were constantly breaking through the ground, and every time they did she seemed to sink a bit deeper beneath the surface.

"Mom!"

"Don't stop!"

But Taylor could go no farther. The earth had swallowed everything below her knees. No matter how hard she tried, she could no longer pull her feet free.

Frantic, she looked back and saw her mother had fallen some twenty feet behind. The powerful ooze had consumed everything beneath her waist.

Strangely, it was only now that Taylor recognized the black dress her mother was wearing. It was the last thing she'd ever worn.

It was the dress she'd been buried in.

"What did you do?" Karen cried.

"I'm sorry, Mom! We were only trying to help!" Taylor heard the words, but they didn't feel like they were really hers. It was like someone was speaking for her. "We didn't know this would happen!"

"Yes you did!" Karen's voice was suddenly angry and shrill. Just as it had filled Taylor's heart with warmth in the library, now it left her with an incredible feeling of dread. "You knew better! You *knew* this would happen! *Wesley told you!*"

Taylor watched the pack approach. They had slowed considerably. The wolves were saving their strength for the business at hand. They sniffed the air, tongues dashing in-and-out of their mouths as they began to circle their prey.

"I'm sorry, Mom! Please! Believe me!"

"You should have listened, little girl! You–"

The wolves attacked before she could finish.

Taylor squeezed her eyes shut, but there was nothing she could do to counter the sound of her mother's heartbreaking scr–

❖ ❖ ❖

Taylor woke with a start, sitting up and casting her blankets onto the floor. Her heart raced. Her brow was wet with sweat. It took her eyes a moment to adjust to the darkness. It was a moment longer before she understood everything that had just happened was only a dream.

She looked the room over, hoping sight of the familiar would return her sense of security. Instead, her eyes fell on the aged paperback laying on her nightstand.

The Wonderful Wizard of Oz.

A classic loved the world over.

Her mother's copy.

Only it wasn't her mother's copy. Not anymore. It wasn't a classic either. She and Wesley had made sure of that.

Taylor leapt from her bed. She grabbed the book and tossed it across the room with a quiet scream. She was back in bed just as quickly, pulling the sheet over her head and closing her eyes.

An hour later, when she finally had the courage to look again, Taylor saw the book had landed with its cover facing the bed. If she couldn't bring herself to walk across the room and move it again, the

Wicked Witch would be there all night, waiting, watching her sleep, watching her every move.

CHAPTER 2

AFTER SEARCHING MOST of the house, Rhonda Bates found her son in the last place she expected. "What are you doing in here?" she huffed. "You're supposed to be getting ready for school."

Wesley sat on his knees in the hall closet, both feet tucked beneath his backside as he dug through a plastic storage bin. There were CDs and DVDs scattered in messy piles all around him.

"I *am* ready," he said matter-of-factly.

"Have you eaten?"

He didn't respond.

"Let's go. I'll pour you a bowl before I leave."

Wesley followed his mom down the stairs and into the kitchen where Wesley's little brother was sitting in a highchair near the table in the kitchen's breakfast nook. He held a blue bowl in one hand and a plastic spoon in the other. Tiny O's of cereal were floating in a pool of milk he'd dumped onto the tray in front of him.

"Ugh! Danny! I don't have time for this!" Rhonda shot a look over her shoulder at Wes. "I hope you know you're cleaning that up."

"What?" Wesley whined. "He's your baby!"

Rhonda rolled her eyes. "Upstairs." She pulled some paper towels from the roll hanging above the kitchen sink then balled them up in her hand. "What were you doing up there anyway? I can't remember the last time I saw you watch a DVD. You download everything nowadays."

"Oh," Wesley began. "That... I just... I need a movie for school." It wasn't the biggest lie in the world. He *did* plan on shoving the DVD into his backpack once he found it. He *did* plan on taking it to school.

"What movie?"

"*The Wizard of Oz*," Wesley said tentatively.

His mom began wiping Danny's spilled cereal back into its bowl.

"Do we have that?"

"You got me the box set for Christmas. Remember?"

"Wes, you've got so many movies, sometimes it's a little hard to keep track."

Wesley furrowed his brow.

It's The Wizard of Oz, he thought. *Who forgets that?*

"So are you still upset about last night?"

Wesley wasn't ready for the conversation to shift subjects but wasn't about to push his luck. It had been a tricky twenty-four hours. It's not every day your parents get a call from the police because their son's gone missing.

"Not really. Are you?"

Rhonda shook her head. "You wouldn't believe the things that were running through my head. I was sure you were trapped in some pervert's basement. Next time this happens–"

"It won't."

"Good." His mother took a moment to think about the words to come. "About that other thing. I know she's your friend, but I think it's time you start building some friendships with other kids."

"Wait. You were serious about that?"

"It was great having Taylor next door when we moved in, but it's been nine months. It's time to move on."

"Why?"

Rhonda sighed. "You know why."

But he didn't. She was forbidding him to spend time with the girl because they'd gotten into trouble one time. It didn't make any sense.

“I know it doesn't seem fair. I get it. But it's not like you'll never see her again. You'll see her on the bus and in school. You just need to branch out and find some kids who are... more like you.”

What the heck does that *mean?* he thought quietly to himself.

Rhonda kissed him gently on the forehead and started out of the room. “Will you keep an eye on Danny until your dad gets out of his shower?”

“Sure. But Mom?”

“Yeah?”

“You've seen *The Wizard of Oz*, right?”

She stopped just shy of the doorway and shook her head.

“Wes? I don't know. I–”

“It's for school.”

It was definitely a lie, but it was a lie that had grown in importance since he'd first told it. Wes had a wild theory about his trip into Oz with Tay, that maybe their actions in Oz had had consequences that stretched beyond the page. Last night it had been a thought so crazy he couldn't even share it with Taylor. But the evidence was beginning to pile up.

"Maybe. What's it about?"

"You know? Dorothy? Toto? Follow the yellow brick road?"

Rhonda turned to go. "Doesn't ring a bell. Maybe we can watch it tonight. Unless Ms. Easton calls again. That happens and you better disappear for good."

❖ ❖ ❖

Taylor stood atop the staircase and sniffed the air. The smell of something sweet and smoky was wafting through her house.

Pancakes, she told herself. *Maybe he's not as mad as I thought.*

The dream was still weighing on Taylor. She hadn't slept well. She was tired, and her mood was dark. But maybe her dad could do something about that. He hadn't said a word since picking her up from the library, but at least he wasn't going to send her to school without breakfast. That was a good sign. Plus, her dad had a way of saying things that made her laugh when she needed it most. If anyone could help her forget about the awful dream she'd had, it was him.

She put on a happy face and hurried down the steps, hopping off the third and skipping the last two. From there it was down the hall, around the corner, and into the kitchen where she found her father stacking dishes in the sink.

Tay faked a yawn and stretched like she'd just crawled out of bed. "Morning."

"Food's getting cold. Why don't you grab a plate?"

"I can't. Already brushed. See?" Taylor bared her teeth in a cartoonish grin. She hoped the goofy smile might get a rise out of her dad and left it hanging in the air like the toothy grin on Wonderland's Cheshire Cat. Unfortunately, when he did finally turn to greet her, he barely acknowledged the smile at all.

"I guess you'll have to brush them again. Sit down."

Taylor trudged across the kitchen and took a plate from the cabinet before slumping down in a chair at the table. She'd been right. There were pancakes waiting – butter, syrup, and a small bowl of berries too. It was the usual spread, but after digging in Taylor began to notice that a few things were a bit... off.

Her dad bought stick butter. Swore by the stuff. Karen had turned him onto it shortly after they met, and now he refused to buy anything else. But this morning's butter came in a red-and-white tub with the grocery store's logo emblazoned across its side. It was no big deal. For Taylor, butter was butter. She never understood why her dad insisted on the expensive stuff. The store brand was just as good. It was just... different.

But then, there was the syrup.

Taylor was used to pouring syrup from a cut-glass pitcher her father warmed in the microwave. It was a quick ritual that made breakfast special, and it was usually enough to get their day off to a good start. But this morning there was no pitcher, and the syrup was just as different as the butter. This new stuff came in a plastic jug and tasted bitter on her lips. Even worse, it left a gritty film on her teeth that she couldn't clean off no matter how many times she swiped them with her tongue. Not that Taylor was going to complain. Not today, at least. She shoveled a big bite of dry pancake into her mouth and chased it with a piece of bacon before finally deciding to test the waters and see just how much trouble she was in.

“I'm probably gonna stop by Wesley's after school. Is that okay?”

Her father stopped washing dishes. His shoulder slumped into a frown.

“I know it usually wouldn't be a big deal, but after last night–”

“The Bates don't want you to spend any more time with their son.”

Taylor's jaw dropped. *“What?”*

Tay’s father turned to face her. He balled up his soiled dishtowel and tossed it onto the counter. “They called late last night after you'd gone to bed. Rhonda asked that I make sure you don't spend nearly as much time with Wes as you have been.”

“What did you say?” Her tone demanded an answer. She wasn't worried about the hole she was digging anymore.

“What did you *want* me to say, Taylor?” He leaned back against the counter. Taylor saw he was wearing the blue overalls he'd worn to the library. Normally clean and perfectly pressed, today they were wrinkled like they'd spent the night on the floor next to his bed. She moved her gaze to meet his once more. His face was long and unshaven, his eyes tired.

Again, things were... off.

"You'll just have to give it some time. For now, just give Wes a little space."

"But that's crazy! Mrs. Bates loves–"

"Your teacher called the police!"

Taylor winced at the tone of his voice. It was eerily similar to the timbre her mother's voice had taken in her dream.

"Is it really that hard to believe there might be repercussions this time?"

"What do you mean *this time*? And why's she assume this was *my* fault?"

He looked at her sideways. Taylor suddenly understood Wesley's mom wasn't the only one who blamed her for what happened. Tay's father did, too. It was in his eyes.

"Wesley's a good kid. He's never in trouble. He's on the honor roll. He's–"

"I'm on the..." Her words trailed off. She was poised to point out the "A" papers hanging on their refrigerator door as proof she and Wesley were one and the same. But when she looked at the fridge all she found were a few letter-shaped magnets there to hold her dad's notes and bills in place. Her school papers – papers that had been there yesterday, papers that had *always* been there – were gone.

Off was no longer the word.

Something was *wrong*.

"What?" he scoffed. "The honor roll? I don't think we get to call you an honor student just because you made straight A's in the first grade. That ship may have sailed, baby girl."

Taylor's eyes were swimming in tears. Her father let out a quiet sigh.

Thank god, she thought. The worst was over. He would sit down beside her, put a comforting hand on her shoulder, and–

He turned to finish the dishes.

Taylor couldn't believe it. She was beginning to wonder if she was actually awake or if this was all part of some nightmare that was never going to end.

"Dad?" She wiped her tears before they fell.

"Yeah?"

"Can we get the stick butter next time?"

He exhaled a quiet groan. "Is that really what you're worried about right now?"

"I know it's expensive, but it reminds me of Mom."

"Me too."

"Do you miss her?"

"Of course," he said. "She was always better at this stuff than me. Truth is, girl, I just don't know what to do with you anymore."

CHAPTER 3

WESLEY WAS WAITING on the corner when Taylor came out of her house and onto the porch. Given the morning she'd had, it was a welcomed surprise. Wes normally waited to see the bus turn into their neighborhood before leaving his house. It was one of those little tricks he'd learned: the less time spent alone on the corner, the less likely he'd be to have an ugly run-in with a bully like Randy Stanford.

"Wow!" It was all he said when she was done telling him about her rocky morning. "I knew my mom was mad, but–"

"You knew? Why didn't you tell me?"

"I didn't think she was serious! She was upset. Parents say crazy stuff all the time, right?"

"You have no idea."

Wesley shifted the weight of his backpack from one shoulder to the other. "How weird was he acting? Scale of one to ten."

"A million? I don't know. It wasn't just him. It was everything. His clothes, his face... breakfast. He's so mad he took my papers off the fridge. *Who does that?*"

Wesley stepped toward her. "This is really important. I need you to think, okay? Did you actually *see* him throw the papers away?"

"No, but–"

"Did you see them in the trash?"

"They were on the fridge yesterday. Where else would he–"

He cut her off. "What if they *weren't*?"

Taylor stared at him blankly.

"Did you bring your copy of *Oz*?"

Taylor had a stack of folders and books held against her chest. She adjusted the stack and pulled her mother's book from a purple folder and handed it to Wesley. He quickly began to flip through its pages.

"At first, I thought it was no big deal. It was strange seeing our picture in The Librarian's book, but it's not exactly the weirdest thing we've seen." Wesley saw the story in her paperback had changed just as it had in the leather-bound tome that was weighing down his backpack. He offered it as his first piece of evidence. "But when you told me about *this* – *this* changed everything. I woke up early this morning to see if my *Wizard of Oz* movie was different, too."

"Was it?"

"I couldn't find it."

Taylor smirked. "Movies get lost all the time."

"See? I knew you'd say that. So I asked my mom. Guess what? She hasn't even *heard* of *The Wizard of Oz*." Wes dug a folded piece of paper from his pocket and handed it over. "I did an internet search after she left. There *isn't* a *Wizard of Oz* movie. It was never made."

He paused to let his statement sink in. Tay scanned the printout of his search.

"I don't care, Wes."

"What?"

Taylor used the paper to gesture toward her house. "Right now I need to fix my *life*. I can't get in any more trouble. This stuff is sad, but–"

"What if it's all connected?"

"It's not."

Taylor watched as Wesley worked to collect his thoughts.

"*The Wizard of Oz* was your mom's favorite book, right?"

She nodded a quick confirmation as Wesley hurried on.

"So do you think it would *still* be her favorite?" He pointed to the paperback cradled with her schoolbooks. "Is that the kind of story she would read to a six-year-old before bed?"

Taylor shrugged. "So what?"

"For most people it's just one less movie in the closet. Most people don't even know there *is* an *Oz* book. But *Oz* changed your mom's life. What kind of person would she have been if you took that away? What kind of person would *you* be? Would she have become an English teacher without that book? If she wasn't a teacher, would you have become the same student?"

The image of the bare refrigerator flashed behind her eyes.

"Maybe we did more than change the story." Wes motioned to their surroundings with outstretched arms. "Maybe this is what our world looks like without it."

Taylor looked away in frustration. It was only now that she noticed her lawn, usually neatly kept and manicured, was growing wild. Even that was different. She felt lost. The world was changing all around her. She even felt like she needed a compass to navigate her emotions. Was she angry? Sad? Was it guilt she was feeling? She couldn't tell, but it all seemed like more than she could handle.

It felt like the wolves were descending on her again.

Part of her wished they were.

"What the heck is this?" a cocky voice called.

Both kids looked up to find Caleb leading a trio of boys toward them.

"You slummin' it, Tay?"

Taylor eyeballed Caleb with disgust. "Not today, Rodriguez. I'm not in the mood."

Caleb raised his hands into the air. "Wow! Take a pill, man. Seriously! It's just... since when do we hang out with Wes Weakly?"

Taylor recoiled. And it wasn't the way Caleb had called her friend Wes Weakly that put Tay on her heels. She was used to that. Wes Weakly was one of the uninspired nicknames Randy had doled out to kids he deemed beneath him, like Double-Wide Wendy or Ally Asthma. Instead, it was the way Caleb said "we" that worried her. *Since when do we hang out with Wes Weakly?* Or, *You're one of us, Tay. What're you doing with this geek?*

Did Caleb Rodriguez actually think that he and Taylor were friends?

Before she could give it much thought, Caleb had his hand cocked, ready to slap Wesley across the back of his head. Instinctively, Wes spun just enough to evade the attack then pinned Caleb's hand behind his back and shoved him away.

Taylor laughed when she saw all three boys take a step back. "You might want to check with Randy before you try putting your hands on my boy," she explained. "Things have changed around here."

Her smile melted when she heard the words come out of her mouth.

"Your boy?" Caleb muttered. "Whatever." He and his friends took a spot near the curb just a few feet away. "Where is Randy, anyway?"

Taylor and Wes exchanged a knowing look. Neither knew where Randy was, but both knew exactly where they'd left him: in Oz.

A yellow school bus rounded the corner. The brakes squealed as it stopped for the kids to climb aboard. Wesley motioned for Caleb and his friends to go first, flashing a sarcastic grin for Caleb as they went. When the others were gone, he turned to face Tay.

"We're going to fix this. Okay? Whatever it is, even if I'm wrong. We'll go back and tell The Librarian everything. He'll know what to do."

She nodded, forcing a grin for Wes. He smiled and turned to get on the bus.

Taylor was lost, but she'd found her compass.

Wesley Bates was the only thing in the world that still felt like home.

CHAPTER 4

THE LIBRARIAN STEPPED from the cave he'd been using as shelter through the night. The sun was finally up, though it couldn't be seen through low cloud cover that stretched across the sky like a child's dingy blanket.

The old man secured the potions and powders kept in his satchel then tossed the bag across his shoulder and took up his staff, ready to begin his journey once more. His bones ached, but The Librarian had quickly found a trek through Oz to be far more agreeable during the day. Not only had it been difficult to find a trail beneath the night's moonless sky, but much of The Librarian's night had been spent hiding from prowlers that now seemed to own the Oz night.

And then, of course, there'd been the screams.

Following his arrival, the darkness had come alive with occasional shrieks from frightened or suffering people nearby. Some in Oz were in more pain than The Librarian could possibly imagine. Their screams became a constant companion as he tracked the Stanfords. Even when he had finally yielded to exhaustion and found refuge in a dark cave, the screams never left him. They just followed him inside and echoed through his dreams.

Uncertain how much safety the morning light would bring, The Librarian fought hunger and walked for hours without a break. He only stopped occasionally to study the dried vegetation at his feet for any signs of a trail left by Douglas, Randy, or their dark friend. At times, he worried he'd lost the trail completely only to later stumble across a sneaker print in the dirt or a broken tree branch. He was relentless in his search. He scoured every inch of earth until the forest gave way to a clearing and he had an opportunity to see what had become of the iconic yellow brick road.

Sadness washed over him as he moved into the barren meadow. The road had been damaged outside the Tin Man's cabin, but not like this. Here, there was nothing left but a black trench twisting through the meadow where the road had been. The Librarian slowed his approach as he grew closer. There were several areas near the trench where the ground was covered in a thin layer of golden powder. They stood out as the only splash of color for miles, and yet, the old man couldn't take his eyes from the muddy trench. It was like a black snake laying in wait, resting as if it had spent the night consuming half of Oz and only needed a short break before it could finish the job.

◆ ◆ ◆

Taylor was looking toward Randy's empty desk when the late bell rang and Mr. Clark marched into the room.

"Good morning!"

His students greeted him with a chorus of groans.

"I know, I know. You missed me more than you can possibly express. You just can't find the words." He winked at Wesley in the front row then took a black marker from his desk and turned toward the white board on the wall behind him. "Unfortunately, yesterday's field trip was only a one day reprieve. That's all you get. It's back to the salt mines today." He went to work, reading his words aloud as he wrote them. "The pen... is mightier... than the sword. Who can tell me what this means?"

A boy in a striped soccer jersey answered without raising his hand. "Isn't that what The Joker said right before stabbing that guy in the neck with one of those big feather pens?"

The room erupted with laughter. The classroom was decorated with comic book memorabilia: bobble heads, posters, framed art, and books. The boy was pointing at a poster of The Clown Prince of Crime near the door.

"Not exactly what I was looking for, Shawn. But I'll give you points for trying."

"Extra credit points?"

"*Cool points.* You need as many of those as you can get."

Shawn waved him off. The kids laughed.

"Anyone else?"

Taylor was paying little attention until she saw Wesley's hand go up in the air.

"Yeah? Wes."

"It means one guy with a sword can only do so much – he can only fight one guy at a time – but if a writer's good enough, maybe he can inspire a thousand guys to pick up a sword and fight for him."

"Okay?" Mr. Clark said. "I *think* I'm with you. Can you take that a bit further?"

Wesley pursed his lips, thinking. "The written word can change the world?"

A few students snickered.

Mr. Clark kept his eyes fixed on Wes. "Kinda corny, don't you think?"

"Well," Wesley stammered. "Not really, no."

A sly grin split the teacher's face. "Me neither. And for those who think it is, you might want to consider this example." The kids watched as he wrote two words on the board: *Common Sense*. "Let's find out who did the reading." He pointed at Shawn. "Who's Thomas Paine?"

Shawn let out an exasperated groan. "Umm... well... he's that guy... that guy who did that thing."

"I take it back. Maybe you *do* need the extra credit." There were giggles again, but the teacher was quick to cut them short. "Anyone else?"

Taylor did a double-take. Wesley's hand was up again.

"Nice! Wesley, go."

"Thomas Paine wrote *Common Sense*."

"Dang!" Shawn blurted. "I was gonna say that!"

"Sure you were," Mr. Clark said.

"It was on the tip of my tongue." Shawn smiled when his quick response earned scattered laughter from the girls in class.

"Wes, take a minute to educate our friend."

Wesley turned in his desk to face Shawn. Taylor couldn't believe how ready he was to embrace the moment. It wasn't like him to participate in class like this. Everyone knew he was a great student, but answering questions in class only drew attention to the fact, something Wesley was normally loath to do.

"Before the American Revolution, this guy, Thomas Paine, he wrote a book called *Common Sense*." Wes paused, thinking. "See, some people were already beginning to think about independence. George Washington, Thomas Jefferson. Guys like that. Founding Fathers. But most weren't. Ordinary people in the colonies were upset with their king, sure, but they didn't know how bad things really were. Even worse, they didn't think they could do anything about it." He pointed to Mr. Clark's writing on the board. "*Common Sense* changed all that."

Mr. Clark took it from there. "*Common Sense* sold more than half a million copies. It spread like wildfire. Everyone was reading it. Within a year, Americans were ready to give their lives to be free of England's rule." He softened his voice. "Can you imagine what your life would be like without *Common Sense*? Would America even be here today?"

"Oh! That's bull!" Shawn interrupted. "We woulda fought back eventually."

"You're probably right. Like Wesley said, the Founding Fathers were already putting the wheels in motion. But if Paine doesn't write *Common Sense*, then we don't have as many able-bodied men signing up to fight. I'm sure we still would have *fought* the American Revolution, I'm just not sure we would have *won*."

Mr. Clark scanned the room. Many of his students were wearing blank expressions, indifferent to the discussion. A few near the back were whispering amongst themselves. "Maybe you guys need something a little more personal. What about Batman, Shawn? Can I convince you *he* changed the world?"

Shawn rolled his eyes, but Mr. Clark was undeterred. He walked across the room and took a framed comic from the wall. "I bought this when I was eight years old. I'd never read anything on my own, but with this one issue I was hooked. Comics, books, short stories, poems – I read anything I could get my hands on."

Wesley eyed the comic with great interest. The cover's illustration had a muscular man in a mask holding Batman over his knee. "Is that the one where Bane breaks Batman's back?"

Mr. Clark arched an eyebrow then handed the piece to Wes. "Not bad." He turned to face Shawn once more. "I might have to give *him* extra credit for that one."

Shawn smirked and dismissed them both with a wave.

"You see, that may not *sound* like a big deal. After all, comic nerds are born everyday. But Batman led me to Sherlock Holmes, Holmes led me to Dickens. By the time I was sixteen I was sending stories I'd written to publishers in New York, begging them for a chance to see my stuff in print alongside the work I loved."

Taylor wasn't surprised to see just how closely Wes was inspecting the old comic or just how intently he was listening to Mr. Clark's tale. She knew he was already firing emails off to editors in New York. They hadn't responded, though. Not yet.

"Of course, that didn't work," Mr. Clark explained. "But I kept trying. I studied English in college, and in my senior year, I sold a few stories to a magazine no one's heard of. When I graduated I took a job that let me—"

"So what?" Shawn interrupted, his tone one of complete disdain. "You're saying you wouldn't be our teacher if it weren't for some stupid comic? C'mon! You think you're the only English teacher who wants to be a writer?"

Mr. Clark was about to respond, but Wesley didn't give him the chance. "You gonna shoot down everything the man says? You act like you've never had a book change your life before?"

Shawn signaled irritation with a noise that made it sound like he was sucking on his own teeth. "Please! You're the bookworm loser around here, Bates."

Taylor snapped to attention. She was ready to jump to Wesley's defense, but Wesley spoke up before she could.

"You go to church, Shawn?"

"Every Sunday," he nodded defiantly. "Play second base for the softball team, too. So what?"

Wesley pushed his glasses up on his nose. "I just wonder if your mom would lay out those cute, little church suits for you if it weren't for a little book called – oh, I don't know – *The Bible*!"

There was a collective gasp. Every kid in the room was shocked that Wesley was able to fire back so quickly. Taylor watched as a wave of amusement washed the room over. Kids were laughing, loudly this time. A moment later, a redhead in the seat beside Shawn was there to rub it in.

"Man, Bates *burned* you!"

Shawn punched the kid in his arm, but the redhead didn't mind. All he did was rub his arm and snicker some more.

"That's a great example," Mr. Clark said. "In fact, it's probably the best example."

He was ready to press on with his lecture but sputtered a bit when the door opened and the school's principal walked into the room. A few whispering students immediately straightened in their seats. A pair of daydreaming kids instinctively picked up pencils like they were ready to take notes. Just the principal's presence was enough to shift everyone's attention where it belonged. Only Taylor was brave enough to watch Principal Dill in the doorway, finally looking away when their eyes met and the tall man frowned.

"It doesn't matter what you believe," Mr. Clark continued. "Books like the *Bible*, the *Koran*, the *Torah* – these religious texts have inspired peace, they've inspired war. They've inspired people to do great things, and they've inspired people to do incredible evil." He centered himself behind the podium. "Every person in this room has been influenced by the written word. What books have influenced your life?"

Wesley stole a look at Taylor across the room. She could already tell he was going to use Mr. Clark's lecture against her the next time he brought up his ridiculous theory about their trip to Oz.

"For some of you, I'm sure an influence will be hard to find. But I think most of you will find that your life has been influenced by the written word more than you think." He raised a finger to let the kids know they'd be taking a short break. "Excuse me a moment."

Most kids shuffled in their seats, moving to talk with a neighbor while they waited. Taylor didn't, though. It was strange, the principal showing up in the middle of class like this. And then, there was the way he had frowned at her.

He's not here for you. He doesn't even know your name.

She began to doodle in the margin of her notes, but it was a distraction that couldn't hold her attention long. A few moments later, she looked up again. This time both Mr. Clark and Principal Dill were looking right at her. It was unmistakable. Taylor surveyed the room. Her classmates suddenly seemed reluctant to make eye contact with her. Everyone looked away when Taylor's eyes landed on them except Wes. Sitting just a few feet from the door, Wesley caught her attention and mouthed a silent message. She couldn't read his lips. All she could make out was the very last word.

Blah-blah-blah...

Something-something-something...

You.

Mr. Clark looked away from his conversation with the principal. "Taylor? Can we talk with you a moment?"

She was hesitant but stood from her desk and slowly started toward them.

"Oh," Principal Dill said in a deep voice. "You might want to bring your things."

Taylor's throat tightened when she saw the tiny piece of blue paper in the principal's hand. She looked to Wesley for help but saw he was nervous, too.

"It's okay," she whispered. "I'll be alright."

She collected her things and followed the two men into the hallway. A few minutes later, Mr. Clark returned.

Taylor didn't.

CHAPTER 5

WESLEY WAITED NEAR Taylor's locker until the warning bell rang and traffic in the hallway began to thin. A few feet away, Old Man Riley was lecturing a lanky boy who couldn't open his locker. The school's maintenance man, Riley had a long pair of orange-handled bolt cutters in hand and was ready to free the locker of its lock.

"Better get to class," someone suggested. Wesley turned to find Ms. Easton hurrying down the hall, the click of her heels echoing against the tile floor. "You don't want to give Ms. Tanner a heart attack like the one you gave me."

She gave him an amused look as she walked by. Wes quickly followed.

"Ms. Easton? Do you know what happened to Taylor? Mr. Dill pulled her out of class with a... *with a blue pass.*" He was trying to hide the worry in his voice but couldn't. Every kid in Astoria Middle School knew having your name scrawled across that little square of blue paper was bad news. Being hand delivered by the principal only made it worse.

"Probably lucky he wasn't there for you both after the stunt you pulled."

"I know," he said. "I'm sorry."

They rounded the corner into the seventh grade hall.

"Well, you didn't hear this from me, but Taylor didn't show up for ISS this morning. Just went straight to class like she wasn't in any trouble at all."

Wesley came to an abrupt halt.

ISS.

In School Suspension.

The final step before expulsion.

Taylor was about to be kicked out of school.

He started after Ms. Easton again. "Why would Tay have ISS?"

"Why *wouldn't* she?" Ms. Easton chuckled. Wesley couldn't tell if she was laughing at his question or Taylor. Either way, the quiet snicker didn't sit well with Wes.

"Is it because we got lost in the library?"

"*Disappeared*, you mean?" She waited for his answer then stopped when she saw Wesley was too nervous to make eye contact. "How did you two hook up? That was... well... *unexpected.*"

"Well, we–"

"You can tell me if she threatened you, Wes."

"*What?* No!"

"She doesn't have to know. You just tell me what happened, and we'll make sure–"

"Tay would never!"

Ms. Easton sighed then started down the hall again. "Taylor has been in-and-out of ISS all year. We only let her go on yesterday's field trip because we were hoping she had turned over a new leaf. Turns out that was wishful thinking, so back in the basement she goes."

Wesley shook his head. Taylor had never even been threatened with ISS, but Wes knew he'd be wasting his breath if he tried to explain. It was clear she didn't know the Taylor Morales he knew. No one did. Not anymore.

"You need to be careful. You're a good kid, Wes. All the teachers love you, but after yesterday we're going to be watching you a little closer. Taylor's got a reputation around here. Had it long before you came. Don't let her pull you down. You've got a bright future ahead of you. You're too good for a girl like that."

She tussled his hair then disappeared into a rowdy classroom nearby.

Wesley felt his stomach churn.

Taylor's got a reputation?

Yeah, for being a teacher's pet.

Old Man Riley came around the corner pushing a cart with a hodgepodge of his tools and supplies. Straggling students were hurrying through doors and into classrooms, the scurry of their feet causing fallen papers to flutter along the tile floor.

Wesley turned to study the staircase leading into the basement at the end of the hall. It was dark, the only part of the hall that wasn't bathed in the natural light flooding through the hallway windows and into the school.

She must be scared to death, Wesley thought.

Riley muttered something beneath his breath about flooded toilets and rotten kids. He had orange hair in his ears and a mouth full of crooked teeth. Most kids were scared to death of the man, but Wesley had always felt sympathy for the old guy. Like The Librarian, there were urban legends about Old Man Riley told in hushed tones all through Astoria – only the Riley stories weren't nearly as nice.

Wesley stepped aside, allowing the maintenance man to shuffle by. Riley grunted another complaint beneath his breath, but Wesley missed it. Something on the cart had caught his eye and sparked a crazy idea.

You're gonna rip me a new one, Tay.

The late bell sounded, and Wesley took off down the hall. Strangely, he didn't turn into one of the noisy classes. Instead, he quietly inched into an empty computer lab, making sure he was alone before heading straight for the teacher's desk.

❖ ❖ ❖

The school's basement was dark and smelled of sulfur. Long lights hung from the ceiling, but most of the fluorescent bulbs had burned out long ago. All that remained were a few that flickered dimly.

Taylor sat in one of a dozen desks that faced the front of the room. While it was set up to look like an ordinary classroom, the basement was anything but. The floor beneath them was stained concrete, and the ceiling above was nothing more than a checkerboard of exposed wires and iron beams. The room was crowded, its walls lined with items being stored until needed by the student body above: the good kids.

Perhaps most telling was the man sitting behind the teacher's desk. He wasn't teaching the kids in ISS. He wasn't working on his lesson plan. He had his feet up and was hiding behind the morning's newspaper. He looked up occasionally when it was time to turn the page, but that was all. He wasn't there to teach.

He was on guard duty.

Taylor adjusted in her seat, using the movement as an opportunity to slyly look the room over. There were four other kids in ISS with her: three boys from her grade and a heavy-set girl from the grade above. In the corner, two of the boys were using a pocketknife to cut an empty soda can in half. When finished, each took a piece of the can for himself and began to spit into the open container that remained. Taylor couldn't take her eyes away. Was it a game? Was it supposed to be fun? Perplexed, she continued to watch as the boys spat one quick loogie after another as if they were racing to see who could fill his half of the can first.

The lights flickered, and the room turned dark. When the cold glow of light returned, Taylor saw one of the boys was looking up at her. He had stubble on his chin and a cigarette tucked behind his ear. It was Russ Kelley.

Supposedly, Russ had been given ISS because he hit Principal Dill across the face with a computer keyboard. When he saw Taylor was watching he snorted loudly then spit into his can once more. She turned away. A few second later, she heard him repeat the disgusting display and winced.

Taylor had never believed the rumors about Kelley's exploits, but it was clear his offense had been serious enough. He'd been in ISS since the first grading period, and the school year was almost up. She'd forgotten all about him.

She looked down and saw someone had carved an obscenity into her desk.

How long before people start forgetting about me? she asked herself. *Maybe they already have.*

Only that wasn't it. Wesley was right. Somehow, the world *had* changed. Things were off. Who knows? Maybe in this strange, new world Russ Kelley really had assaulted their principal. Or maybe it had been something worse.

The legs on the teacher's chair squeaked as he pushed back from his desk. “I'll be right back,” he explained. “No one's to move from their seat. Understood?”

Russ and his friend focused their attention on Taylor as their teacher started for the door. Both grinned wickedly. Taylor swallowed hard. Her palms began to sweat. She didn't belong down here with these guys. Definitely not alone. What if they tried something once the teacher was gone? What if–

“Mr. Marsh?”

Taylor turned to find Wesley standing in the doorway. He was handing the teacher a pink piece of paper cut into a small rectangle: an office pass.

“What's this?” Mr. Marsh grumbled.

“I'm supposed to bring her upstairs.”

“She just got here. What's going on?”

“They don't tell me that,” Wesley explained. He turned to look Taylor in the eye. “I think *her mom* is here to bring her home.”

Mr. Marsh flapped a hand in her direction before heading out the door. “Looks like you’re on early release, Morales.”

Taylor quickly collected her things then took the long way around, navigating through the desks so she wouldn't have to walk past Russ and his friend with their dueling cans of spit.

"What's going on?" she asked nervously.

Wesley didn't answer. He led her down the hall and up the stairs. Tay saw Wes was wearing his backpack. It seemed to bulge more than usual, and there was something orange poking through the opened zipper.

"You're not an office aide," Taylor whispered.

"No kidding."

"And my mom is..." She couldn't say the word. "Why aren't you in math? Where'd you get that pass?"

"I stole it from the computer lab."

"*What?*"

Wesley fired her a cold look to let her know she was being too loud.

"This isn't something you can fix, Wes."

They were atop the staircase now. Wesley peeked around the corner before they stepped into the open.

"It's like the whole world's gone crazy," Taylor said.

"I bet you believe me now, huh?"

"That's what I'm saying. You can't just take me back to class."

"We're not going back to class." Wesley reached over his shoulder, grabbed the orange handles, and slid Old Man Riley's bolt-cutters from his backpack. He started into the hallway. "We're bustin' outta here."

"What are you gonna do with those?"

"Randy rides his bike to school, right?"

Taylor grinned mischievously, finally catching on.

"Hey!" someone yelled. "You there!"

Both kids whipped around.

Old Man Riley was barreling down the hallway toward them, a fist pumping in the air. "Stop! Bring those back! Bring 'em back, I said!"

"Oh, crap!"

Taylor and Wes bolted down the hall.

Ms. Easton came out of her classroom just ahead of them. "What's going on out here?"

"Stop them!"

Taylor slowed her pace when the teacher moved into their path, but Wesley put a hand on her back to keep Tay moving. They rushed right by Ms. Easton before she had a chance to react.

Wesley laughed as they slid around the corner. "And you thought she was a bad influence on *me*!"

The kids led Riley on a zigzag course through the building before they disappeared through a pair of double doors that led to the playground behind the school.

Taylor gestured toward the bolt cutters. "Slow down! You aren't even supposed to run with scissors!" Wesley followed her advice and slowed his pace to a fast walk.

Together, they marched toward a collection of bike racks near the playground and adjacent to the school's parking lot. There were three teachers standing together just outside the playground's border, no doubt there to supervise the small army of elementary students playing nearby.

"Don't look at them," Wesley explained.

"I'm not."

"But don't act like you're *afraid* to look at them."

"Okay."

"Just... walk casual."

"Wes?"

"Yeah."

"Shut up."

They stopped just short of the small area where kids were allowed to park their bikes after riding them to school. There were six metal racks grouped together. Each sat parallel to its neighbor. About a dozen bikes were parked between the bars on each of the racks.

"You know which one's his?"

Wesley's eyes moved to a black mountain bike with silver accents and thick tires safely chained to the last rack. "Of course," he answered dryly. "You know how many times he's tried to run me over with this thing? Idiot calls it the Black Mamba. What a joke."

Wesley let his backpack drop to the ground then stepped toward the bike with the bolt cutters raised. Taylor stole a glance toward the playground. The teachers were still talking amongst themselves. They hadn't noticed Taylor and Wes, and the younger kids were too busy to care.

Taylor spotted a small group of kids playing tug-o-war over a large sandbox. Boys against girls. The battle didn't last long. After a brief struggle, the girls yanked hard enough to pull all three boys face first into the sand. The boys staggered to their feet, laughing as they coaxed the girls into a race for the swings. Taylor smiled wistfully. She missed recess. Life was a lot simpler when she brought a lunchbox to school.

It took most of Wesley's strength, but the chain holding Randy's bike eventually broke with a loud snap. He pulled the chain free with a flourish.

"So begins my life of crime!"

"Who *are* you?" Taylor giggled.

But her nervous laughter quickly disappeared when something occurred to her. Like so much around her, Wesley had changed, too.

Two weeks ago Wesley ate lunch from a tray on his lap in a locked bathroom stall because Randy Stanford tried to make him eat pudding off the cafeteria floor. She couldn't see that happening now. Wes didn't seem like he would hide in the bathroom from anyone. He looked ready to take on the world.

And that's what scared her.

She and Wes were heading back to the library hoping they could make everything go back to normal. And she really wanted things to be normal again. She wanted her syrup warmed. She wanted her papers back on the fridge. She wanted teachers to leave her in charge when they left the room like they normally would. Most of all, she wanted her dad back. Her *real* dad. She'd already lost one parent, now it seemed she'd lost another – only this time it was her fault.

But if she got those things, would Wesley go back to the way *he* had been before? Would he find himself back in that bathroom stall? She didn't think so, but she couldn't be sure.

Her thoughts drifted to the game of tug-o-war, only this time it wasn't boys against girls, it was right vs. wrong. She didn't know if leaving school with Wes was right or wrong, but she had a sneaky suspicion the choices would only get more difficult once they left.

Wesley had Randy's bike free of the rack. He threw one leg over the seat and readied the pedals for take off. "Ready? Let's go."

She climbed onto the bike's pegs, two metal posts, one on either side of the rear tire, positioned there to allow for an added passenger, even if it was standing room only.

Wesley labored to steady the bike and get it going before straightening the handlebars when momentum finally took over. He pedaled down the walk and over the curb. "Hold on!"

Taylor tightened her grip on his skinny shoulders as they banked around the corner and into the parking lot. Wesley was the only part of her life that still felt right. He was the rock she could hold onto, but as they sped out of the parking lot and into the street, Taylor was beginning to wonder if eventually she would have to let this new Wesley Bates go.

CHAPTER 6

WESLEY POUNDED ON the library's wooden doors then yanked on their heavy brass handles in frustration. The doors rattled in their frame but barely gave an inch, clearly locked from the other side. He kicked at them angrily as Taylor walked through the grass to peer through one of the building's tall windows.

"Well?"

"I can't see a thing."

"Great! Who's closed at eleven o'clock in the morning?"

"Maybe they've closed for good." Taylor pointed into the parking lot where several workmen in orange vests were milling about alongside construction equipment and several large dumpsters. Her eyes focused on the tall crane with a wrecking ball hooked to its chain. "I thought they weren't gonna tear this place down until summer."

Wesley started around the corner, careful as he stepped through a flowerbed that bordered the building. "Let's try around back."

Taylor was reluctant but followed all the same. This was starting to feel a lot like trespassing to her. When she found Wesley crouched near a bush trying to pry open a skinny basement window, it felt like something even worse: breaking-and-entering.

"What are you doing?"

"What's it look like? We can't let one locked door stop us. Besides," he came to his feet when the window wouldn't budge, "getting in will probably be the easy part."

Taylor watched Wesley size things up. His eyes gleamed with delight when they landed on one of the large stones at the base of a tree just a few feet away.

"Wes, no."

"Pretty soon this place won't even be here." He knelt beneath the tree, rocked the heavy stone onto its side then struggled to lift it. "Think of this as... early demolition."

"Swiping Randy's bike was one thing," Taylor reasoned. "Actually, that was kinda fun. But this? They've already called the police on us once."

"What else can we do?"

Taylor let her gaze fall. The corner of her lip curled into a small frown. "It's just not right."

"Sometimes we have to do things that aren't right, Tay." His tone was soft yet somehow stern. "How many times have we been told to keep our hands to ourselves? A million? Didn't stop you from cheering when I belted Randy, did it?"

"That was different."

"So is this."

Taylor looked away.

Those kids were playing tug-o-war again.

"Fine," she said. "Just not one of the stained glass windows. They look expensive and old and... too pretty to break."

Wesley had been fighting the rock with both hands, a struggle that left the front of his shirt covered in mud. He lifted the stone, his tiny wrist wavering beneath its weight, then sent it crashing through the glass and into the dark room on the other side. A crooked grin cropped up on his face as he moved to inspect his work, eyes fixed on the jagged glass that remained in the window's frame.

"Careful," Taylor reminded.

Wesley hurried to a nearby tree, broke off a low hanging branch, and used the heavy stick to break the remaining glass from the frame. "There," he said. "Happy?"

"What if someone heard?"

"Then they should have answered the door."

Taylor smirked. "Here, I'll lower you down."

A tinge of worry showed on Wesley's face. "But I thought–"

"I'm still stronger than you, kid. You couldn't hold me if you tried."

Taylor saw hurt in Wesley's eyes and worried she may have gone too far. But Wesley's dismay quickly gave way to an infectious snort. A moment later, they were laughing together.

"Maybe if you laid off the donuts," Wesley joked.

Taylor feigned shock and playfully smacked him across the arm with the back of her hand. "Whatever! Jerk!"

Wesley went down on all-fours then sent his legs through the window, a move that left the entire lower half of his body dangling above the basement floor.

"Can you touch?"

"Not yet," Wesley said. "Give me your hands."

Taylor sat down in front of him and braced her feet against the building's stone exterior before extending both hands for Wesley to take. He took her left first, using his right hand to keep balance so he wouldn't fall. Once he had a firm grip, he lunged forward and grabbed the other hand.

"Dang," she whined. "*I* should lay off the donuts?"

"Shut up and lower me down."

Taylor's face was already turning red as she toiled to hold Wesley in place. She shifted her feet on the wall and straightened her knees, hoping better footing would be enough to ease her efforts. Once anchored, she slowly bent forward at the waist, lowering Wesley through the window toward the–

Wesley's body lurched away from her! Taylor nearly tumbled through the window after him!

"What the heck, Wesley?"

Wesley's eyes widened. He struggled to look over his shoulder into the darkness below. "Something–"

His body jerked down on her again. This time Taylor's knees buckled, and Wesley slid farther into the darkness below. His breathing quickened, tiny gasps coming in short bursts one right after another.

"Pull me up!"

"I got you! Just–"

"SOMETHING'S DOWN THERE! PULL ME UP!"

Taylor tightened her grip, pushing out against the building with her legs, straining as she used every ounce of her strength to pull Wesley up again.

But she lost ground.

Too much of his weight was beneath the window.

She couldn't lift him.

Something below pulled on Wesley again.

"Don't let go!" Taylor yelled. *"Don't–"*

His grip slipped so that they were no longer holding onto one another's wrists. Instead, they were palm-to-palm, fingers slipping the more they squeezed.

"Hold on, Wes! Just—"

There was one final jerk, and Wesley's hands slipped from hers. He disappeared in a flash.

"Wesley!"

She jumped to her feet, looking for help. A rock. A limb. A shovel leaning against the building. Anything that might serve as a weapon against whatever was waiting for them in the library's basement.

She stepped away from the window and drew a deep breath.

"Dang it! Dang it! Dang it!"

Taylor sprang forward, fell to the ground and slid through the grass. She closed her eyes as her feet went through the window, unsure what was waiting in the darkness below, scared to death as she left the outside world and began to fall.

◆ ◆ ◆

Randy stumbled over a jagged stone jutting out of the rocky cliff he and his father were walking along.

"Careful," Douglas said. "It's a long way down."

Randy cautiously looked over the cliff's edge only to find he couldn't see the bottom through the soupy mist clinging to the canyon walls.

"You need a break?"

"No," Randy panted. "I'm fine."

Douglas slowed his pace just enough so the two could walk side-by-side. They traveled in silence for a few minutes, Randy watching as his father occasionally looked back in the direction from which they came.

"Is something wrong?" he asked.

"No. It's just... someone might be following us."

"The Librarian?"

Douglas looked down at him. "Why would you say that?"

Randy shrugged. "Isn't it obvious?"

"Maybe," his father said. "We'll have to see, I guess."

"Is that why you sent him back? To look?"

Douglas grinned. "You're a little scared of Bones, aren't you?"

Randy didn't answer. He couldn't understand why his dad had given the hooded man such a playful nickname.

"It's okay. I imagine *all* of this is a little scary."

"That's just it. I don't know what is going on."

Douglas grinned. "Look around, son. It's right in front of you. You tell me."

"I... I don't know."

"Yes you do. Where are we? I want to hear you say it."

Randy looked about but was hesitant before answering. "We're in Oz."

"Exactly."

"But... but how is that possible?"

"Haven't you ever read a book that just came alive in your head?"

Randy shook his head.

"That's something we've got to change. A good book is better than any video game or movie. Nothing comes close." Douglas put an arm around his son as they continued. "Sometimes reading a book can feel like–"

"Magic?"

"That's right. And there are authors in the world – masters who have learned to *tap into that magic*. Some know they've done it, some don't. But Shakespeare, Bradbury, Poe, Twain: they were wizards with a pen, those rare authors whose words jumped off the page and became real."

Douglas motioned to the Oz landscape around them as if it were all the evidence his son should need. While Randy was beginning to buy in, he still felt like his father was evading the bigger question.

"That still doesn't explain why we're here."

Douglas shifted his gaze, looking down his nose at Randy as if the boy were pressing him a bit too hard now. "The Librarian has something of mine. He promised to give it to me a long time ago but never did."

"What?"

"A book."

Randy scrunched up his brow. "Really? This whole mess is over a book?"

"Yes and no," Douglas explained. "That may not be the best way to describe it. It's not just a book. If a book had a spirit... or a soul... that's what we're after."

"Like... a ghost book?"

"I guess you could call it that."

"What's it about?"

Douglas looked into the distance, thinking. "Us," he said. "It's about us."

Randy furrowed his brow. He knew his dad was trying to explain things, but he felt more lost than ever. "Dad, that doesn't make any sense. A book can't–"

"Finally," Douglas whispered.

Randy followed his father's gaze to see what had stolen his attention. The boy's mouth fell open when he saw what was waiting beyond the canyon on the horizon ahead.

Barely visible through the mist, a dark castle was perched on a stone spire in the distance. Though built of brick and mortar, the strange building looked like the tangled roots of a centuries-old oak. Randy couldn't help but think the building looked alive. Inside, candles lit up the castle windows like tiny eyes looking out into the murk. Its drawbridge entrance was shaped like a mouth, one ready to consume any visitors that dared approach.

"I was beginning to think we were going the wrong way," Douglas confessed.

"That's where we're going?"

"We'll be fine. We'll rest awhile and wait for Bones before going any farther."

Randy couldn't believe he wanted the Headless Horseman to return. He'd seen the villainous visage waiting beneath the dark man's hood, but at least he was on their side. Whatever waited in the castle beyond was unknown; and yet, Randy was sure it was an evil beyond anything that had ever set foot in Sleepy Hollow. He wasn't even sure the chasm between them and the castle was enough to keep them safe.

The little voice in his head was back.

You should have gone back when you had the chance.

It's too late now, Randy.

Too late.

◆ ◆ ◆

The assistant librarian marched Wesley and Taylor up the stairs that led out of the library's basement. She had Taylor by the arm and was pulling Wesley by the ear.

"Oww! Lady, that's my ear!"

"Stop," Taylor whined. "We can explain!"

"I should have known the two of you would show up again," Hope snarled. "Don't you think you've caused enough trouble?"

She forced them onto a long wooden bench in one of the building's dark corridors where she made them sit.

Taylor rubbed her arm. "Doesn't mean you have to be so mean about it! Dang!"

"You just threw a rock through our basement window. How do you *think* I should treat you?" The kids clammed up. "I guess it does pale in comparison to the trespassing offense from yesterday."

"Trespassing?" Taylor was trying to act offended even though the words coming out of Hope's mouth echoed her thoughts from before.

"As if I don't know about your little jaunt into Oz." The kids looked surprised. "Didn't I warn you? I specifically said, 'Don't touch the carvings.'"

"We're here to see The Librarian," Wesley said defiantly.

"Oh? You are? Why didn't you say so?"

Taylor clenched her jaw, and Wesley shook his head. Neither appreciated the woman's sarcastic tone.

"He's not here. After all, someone's got to clean up the mess you made." She turned to walk away. "He left for Oz late last night."

"Wait," Wesley said. "How?"

"Through the carving, kid. Just like you."

Wesley and Taylor came off the bench and hurried after her into the main hall. There was an eerie atmosphere in the library this afternoon. It was empty, and none of the lamps were lit which left most of the building enveloped in shadow. It felt like someone had dropped a black veil over the building.

"That's not what I meant. How's he gonna fix what we did?"

Hope turned to face them. "What exactly did you two do over there?"

Wesley pressed his lips together, unwilling to talk.

"We freed the Tin Man," Taylor whispered in shame.

Hope stabbed Wesley in the chest with an extended finger. "What were you thinking? A kid like you? I thought for sure you'd have more respect for a story than that."

"I do!"

"Oh yeah, I can tell!"

"It's not his fault!" Taylor raised her voice so it could be heard over their bickering. Both stopped the minute the declaration was off her lips. "Wes warned us something like this might happen. Don't yell at him."

The room fell silent.

"Can you tell us what happened?" Wesley asked.

Hope sighed. "You played with toys that don't belong to you. Stories are like puzzles, okay? When a writer sits down he has a million ideas. Some of those ideas fit well together, some don't. Not every idea gets used, but eventually, the writer spends enough time playing with the pieces that a picture comes into focus. He starts to understand what his story is about."

Wesley nodded in agreement. He had a small shoebox in his closet that was filled with stories he'd written, screenplays, even the beginnings of a fantasy novel he planned to finish over summer break. But also in the box, scattered haphazardly throughout, were tiny notes with just a handful of words written on them: his idea slips. Some were story concepts; others were just good lines he wanted to include in his next project; others still were a single word: maybe a place or subject he wanted to tackle in some future work. He'd never thought of them as puzzle pieces, but that seemed an apt metaphor. He usually spent Friday night thumbing through the tiny shreds to decide what he would write about and often found several of the ideas naturally fit together to help create a more complete story.

"Dorothy was meant to kill the Wicked Witch, but if you know the story well enough you know she can't even make it to the Witch's castle without the Tin Man's help. You took away one of the most important pieces of the puzzle. So now, all those pieces? All those story elements you know were taken apart and put back together again. Only this time the picture's just a little bit different, isn't it?"

Hope grinned ruefully. "Still," she began, "I'm guessing that's not enough to make you break out my window. Something tells me you aren't the kind to go around vandalizing private property on a whim."

She saw the kids exchange a look and knew what was being said without hearing the words: *Should we tell her?*

"Let me guess. Life was just a little different out there than you remember?"

Another look traded: *How does she know that?*

Taylor finally spoke up. "Why would the things we did in Oz affect the real world, too?"

"They didn't," Hope explained. "It just seems that way. The school you left this morning? That isn't your school. The bed you slept in last night? Not your bed. Nothing you've seen since leaving the library belongs to you." She looked through the window at the busy street outside. "Your actions in Oz didn't change anything in our world... they took us to a *new* one."

CHAPTER 7

WESLEY STOOD ALONE in the library. He studied the deep intricacies of the Neverland carving and quietly wondered what his wild friend might be doing on the other side.

Strangely, Hope's explanation of recent events had left Wesley feeling like *his side* of the portal was the fantasy, as if Astoria was the make-believe land. He'd read sci-fi novels that dealt with alternate realities, but this whole thing was quite confusing, even for him.

Hope had tried to put it as simply as she could: "When you freed the Tin Man you altered the *Oz* story. Dorothy *never killed* the Wicked Witch. Instead, the Witch killed her. When that happened, the library shifted to a world where Baum wrote *that* ending instead of the one you know. Everything outside these walls is exactly the same except for that one little difference. Of course, you've begun to realize one small difference can have a pretty big effect."

It was the part about the library's shift that was sticking with Wes. He couldn't get past the visual of an old stone castle hurtling through time and space. Wesley spotted a crack in the library's wall. He wondered if the imperfection was there before he and Taylor's trip to Oz or if it was something new.

"It's a lot to process, isn't it?"

Wesley turned to find Hope standing in the aisle behind him.

"Sometimes I wonder if *I* understand everything about this place." She stepped toward Wes. He felt a strong urge to inch away. "I'm sorry I came down on you so hard in there. It's just... this is pretty scary stuff."

"I'm sorry we broke your window."

"Was that your idea?"

"Yeah."

"But it *wasn't* your idea in Oz?"

"It was my idea to *go*."

"That's not so bad. At least you had good reasons for that."

She had changed again. She was soft and kind, almost motherly. *You never know what you're gonna get with this woman*, Wesley thought.

"I understand escaping to Oz because you needed somewhere to hide," she said. "But why did Taylor decide to free the Tin Man? How did *that* happen?"

"What do you mean?"

"Well," Hope began, "you had a good reason for *going*. You were running from someone and scared out of your mind. But why did they insist on freeing the Woodsman? It sounds like you warned them this would happen."

"Not *this*, exactly. But, yeah... something."

"Well, like I said. I'm sorry I came down on you so hard. It doesn't sound like this is your fault at all." She started down the aisle and into the library's main hall. "If your friends had just listened to you we wouldn't even be in this mess."

Wesley watched her disappear around the corner.

Maybe she's not so bad.

He started ambling along, perusing the wall alone, looking at each of the wooden carvings that had enraptured him the day before. It was hard to enjoy them as he had during the field trip with Ms. Easton. Before, they'd been nothing more than cool pieces of art. Now they were something more: powerful relics that demand respect, doors that should only be opened by those who would act responsibly once they've walked through.

She's right, Wesley thought quietly to himself. *Those guys should have listened.*

◆ ◆ ◆

Taylor turned away from the Oz display, shoving one hand behind her back when she heard Hope approach.

"You and Wesley should probably stay here," Hope explained. "You'll want to make sure you're inside these walls when The Librarian does his work in Oz. If not, you might end up stuck in *that* Astoria instead of your own." She pointed a finger at the building's chained entry to indicate the city beyond.

Wesley appeared behind her. "Actually, we had a slightly different plan." He looked over at Tay. "You get it?"

"Yeah. We're good to go." Taylor brought her hidden hand into view. Her fingers were wrapped tightly around the magic wand from the Oz display.

Hope looked stunned. "What do you think you're doing?"

"We're going back," Wesley said.

"No you're not!" Hope tried to snatch the wand from Taylor's hand, but Tay pulled away before she got close.

"You said this was our fault!" Taylor exclaimed. "Now we're gonna fix it."

"Or you'll make it worse."

Wes quickly spoke up. "Have you flipped through a copy of *Oz* this morning? I don't think that's possible." His backpack was sitting atop a stack of books on the library's marble floor. He removed the book The Librarian had given him then handed it over. Hope flipped through it.

"Fine. Let's pretend I let you go back. What then? What are you going to do?"

A lump raised in Wesley's throat. It was the question he hoped no one would ask. He'd come to the library hoping The Librarian could help them, but The Librarian wasn't available. Now it was on him. He knew they had to return to Oz, but he had no idea what to do once there. After all, how can you stop ripples on the water's surface once someone's thrown a rock into the pond?

"Well," he began tentatively, "I'm a writer... well... I'm going to be, at least."

"Wesley's a writer," Taylor said. "A great one."

He smiled. It was just the boost he needed.

"Get to the point," Hope demanded.

"You said it best," Wesley began. "A story is like a puzzle. You need someone who can look at the pieces you've got and figure out how to put them back together."

"And if by some miracle you're able to do that? How are you going to get back?" Wesley didn't know what to say. Hope grinned. "Whoever built these doorways was smart enough to build doors that only swing one way. Otherwise the real world would end up overrun with fictional characters looking to escape their worlds. Coming home won't be nearly as easy as–"

"Locke knows how to get back," Taylor said.

Wesley nodded his head. "That's right."

"I was starting to miss that little guy, anyway."

They started toward the Neverland display. Wesley took Pan's dagger, tossing it from one hand to the next, feeling its weight, checking its balance.

"You think it will be hard to find him?" Wes directed his question to Tay but knew Hope was listening.

Hope tried to interrupt. "Hey?"

"I don't know," Taylor answered. Both children were ignoring the woman's intrusion. "We'll have to see where the portal leads."

"Hey!"

The kids turned. Wesley looked at Hope over the top of his glasses. Taylor put a hand on her cocked hip. This time *they* were the ones acting impatient, as if Hope had worn out her welcome and no longer had anything to add.

"Fine," Hope huffed.

They had her.

"Each Librarian has an amulet. The Watchers, too. They're like keys that allow you to open portals from the other side in case you need to travel into one of the storybook lands. You know? In case something like *this* happens."

"What do the amulets look like?" Wesley asked.

Hope began to fidget. "I don't know."

Taylor fixed Hope with a skeptical stare, but Wesley was beginning to reflect on their meeting with The Librarian the night before. Wes had been so disappointed when a bookmark was the only thing waiting for him in the book The Librarian had gifted him, but he was beginning to think he'd found something more.

Wesley used his thumb to pull the long silk cord from under his shirt. He continued pulling on the cord until the metal bookmark hanging from his neck appeared from inside his collar and fell across his chest.

"Does it look like this?"

The color drained from Hope's face. "Where did you... I thought..." She couldn't finish. Hope lunged toward Wes, a hand out as if ready to snatch the amulet from his neck. "Give me that!" she demanded. "You shouldn't... you don't..." Her voice trailed off. She stopped short of Wesley, perhaps realizing she was about to go too far.

Hope pulled a chair from a nearby table, sat down, and buried her face in both hands.

"What's wrong?" Taylor asked.

Wesley answered for her. "He can't get back."

Hope looked up and pointed at the amulet dangling from Wesley's hand. "Not without that."

Taylor knelt down in front of her. "You want to go back with us?"

CHAPTER 8

AFTER WAITING FOR Bones, Douglas led his trio along the canyon's edge until they came to an ancient rope bridge that traversed the chasm before disappearing into the canyon's thick mist. They crossed carefully, and the old footbridge swayed with every step. When they finally reached its end, Randy saw the bridge had led them to the foot of a towering staircase that spiraled up the rock face toward the castle perched above. The stairs were nearly vertical, each tall step carved from the strange rock formation the castle sat upon.

Randy was breathing heavily just minutes into their climb. His thighs were on fire; his calves felt like they were made of lead. An hour later, when they finally arrived at the summit, he wasn't sure he had any energy left.

Douglas stopped so his son could rest and he could measure what lay before them. A worn path led from the landing atop the stairs to the castle just fifty yards ahead. As intimidating as it had seemed from afar, the castle wasn't nearly as threatening from their current vantage point. Built of roughly-hewn stone, one might even draw comparisons to Astoria's library. Its security was simple, nothing more than a sentry in the tower to keep watch and two guards on either side of the castle's drawbridge entry.

"I expected more," Douglas said. "Wait here."

Randy didn't want to be left behind with Bones but didn't question his father's direction.

Douglas began to meander the path leading to the castle's gate. He had only covered half the distance when the sentry in the tower spotted him.

"Look! There!" The guards began to scramble, arming themselves with long spears before starting toward Douglas. Both were wearing leather armor and strange caps made of fur. "No beggars! Turn and go the way you came!"

"I'm not a beggar," Douglas explained. "I don't want food. I'm here seeking an audience with the Wicked Witch."

One of the guards had a crooked nose. He leveled his spear at Douglas. "Her Highness isn't to be called *Witch*, outsider! Not anymore!"

Douglas bowed his head. "I'm sorry. I misspoke."

"Clearly!"

"But that *is* why I'm here."

"You're a brave one, outsider. No one comes to see Her Highness. She comes to see *you*! And pray she never does!"

Douglas stared back at them.

The crooked-nosed guard pointed the way with his spear. "Turn and go. We'll forget this happened."

"Open the gate," Douglas demanded. "Open the gate and lower the bridge. Now."

Randy watched the guards exchange a dumbfounded look.

Without a word, the lead guard lunged toward Douglas with his spear raised.

Randy darted up the path. "Dad!"

Douglas fixed his eyes on the attack. As soon as it was within reach, he deftly guided the spear away, pulled a pistol from beneath his jacket, and sent two rapid-fire shots into the guard's chest.

Randy stopped, staring in disbelief at the weapon in his father's hand. Everything slowed to a near halt as the unfamiliar roar of gunshots echoed through the countryside. The wounded guard stood motionless, staring at his bloody wounds in utter disbelief. The spear dropped from his hand, and he was next, falling to the ground in a heap beside his weapon.

With that, the world started spinning again.

Randy stumbled up the path toward his father.

The sentry in the tower called for help.

The other guard hurried to his companion's side and examined the fatal wound. "Wha... wha..." The guard was trembling so violently that the metal accents on his armor jangled. *"What have you done?!"*

"I told you," Douglas said. "I've come seeking an audience with Her Highness." His eyes narrowed. "Maybe *you'll* take me to see her... *your Witch.*"

◆ ◆ ◆

Taylor stood outside the Tin Man's cabin. Her throat felt like it was closing up. While she'd expected the worst, nothing could have prepared her for the wasteland that was waiting for them upon their return. This wasn't the Oz she and Wesley had visited. It was her nightmare come to life.

Her gaze fell on the spot in the meadow where she and her mother had met their demise in her dream. A wolf howled in the distance. Taylor shuttered.

"You okay?" Wesley asked.

She answered with a slight nod and a deep breath.

Together, they hurried to catch up with Hope who was walking into the meadow ahead of them. Wesley saw Hope was working the tiny keyboard on a smart phone with her thumbs, typing as they went.

"Do you even have a signal?"

"What?" It was another one of those questions that seemed to catch Hope off guard. "Oh," she stuttered. "It was worth a try, right?" She quickly shoved the phone back into her pocket.

"I guess," Wesley shrugged.

Hope gestured for them to move ahead. "Okay. It's your show. Lead the way."

Both kids were hesitant to take the lead but did so nonetheless. They found the dirt path they'd used before with relative ease, but it was amazing how the woods had changed since their visit. Every tree was bare, long branches reaching into the air like the bony fingers of a skeleton.

The three followed the path on its corkscrew through the dead forest as early evening shadows stretched across the land. Taylor and Wes were both quietly hoping they would find the old woman's cabin before darkness fell, but it wasn't looking good. The sun was descending, and as the shadows grew, blinking eyes began to appear in the tree trunks all around them.

Oz was waking up as the sun went down.

Taylor checked their surroundings as the trees began to stretch like groggy children waking from their slumber. They began to talk amongst themselves as they noticed the humans walking through their forest.

"They don't belong," a tree with white bark murmured.

"Yes they do," another yawned. "I've seen that ugly little girl with the dark skin in our forest before."

Taylor cringed.

"The boy is frail and weak," another continued. This one sounded like a wise, old owl. "He won't survive the night."

"Watch the woman walk," another slurred. "She looks delicious."

Growing worried, they all quickened their pace.

"You sure this is the way?" Hope asked.

"Yeah," Taylor whispered. "Let's just hope they're still here."

"What?"

"We didn't exactly free the Tin Man thinking he would go back to the old woman's house. We were doing it so they could *get away*."

"From what I hear you really weren't thinking at all?"

"What are you talking about? Heard from who?"

Tay shot Wesley a confused look, but he wasn't listening. They'd just crested the hill. His eyes were fixed on the valley below.

"We're back," he said solemnly.

The old woman's cabin looked just as it had before. Everything was exactly as the kids had left it. They passed the well where they'd hid with Locke. Wesley spotted the maiden's axe near the chopping block where she'd labored until her fingers bled. It was amazing how familiar things felt, as if this was the one part of Oz that had gone untouched by the evil that had taken over.

The warm glow of yellow light filled the cabin's windows. "Someone's home," Hope said. "Who's going up?"

Taylor and Wes traded a nervous look and quietly decided they would climb the porch steps together. When they did, the cabin's door crept open with a loud creak before either had an opportunity to knock.

Wesley pushed on the door and slowly stepped into the cabin. "Hello?"

"Wes?" Taylor whispered.

Flickering candles were scattered throughout the cabin. A neatly made bed stood in the corner. A sitting area occupied the space near a window on the opposite side of the room. It was a cozy home, and yet, despite a roaring fire in the cabin's cobblestone fireplace, it felt oddly cold. Something wasn't right, and Taylor was certain it had something to do with the woman sitting on the floor with her legs crossed. Her face was hidden behind a curtain of crinkled grey hair. There was a wooden toolbox on the floor beside her. She had a pile of clunky, metal parts in her lap. There were more parts piled on a table nearby, but Taylor paid them little mind.

Taylor stepped forward. "Ma'am?"

The woman was rocking back and forth, cradling something in her arms like a baby. She mumbled something but didn't look up.

"Ma'am?" Taylor repeated. "Are you okay?"

"Sat on a wall... had a great fall..."

Her words were rhythmic, like a chant or a poem.

Footsteps sounded as someone came onto the porch. Taylor and Wes whipped around to find Hope had finally worked up the courage to climb the steps and was now watching from just inside the door. "That her?"

"Would you be quiet?" Taylor whispered sternly.

The old woman looked up at them. Tears streamed in muddy tracks down her cheeks. Her skin was the lifeless color of spoiled milk. Her eyes were bloodshot, each shadowed by a black circle like the dark side of a crescent moon.

"Are you here to take me away?" The woman let her toothless mouth hang open. Her tongue was pale and bloated like the belly of a dying fish.

“Why would we do that?” Taylor asked. “We're here to help.”

“Oh!” If there was any sign of relief in her voice it quickly gave way to madness. “Good!” She cackled. “Good! Good!” Her boisterous laughter sent a chill down Taylor’s spine. “We could use an extra hand around here!” The old woman tossed the item in her lap toward Taylor who caught it on instinct. “Lord knows he doesn't have one to spare!”

The woman's manic laughter reached a fevered pitch as Taylor looked down to see what she was holding. She turned the silver sphere over, only realizing it was the Tin Man’s head when he saw his metal face staring up at her, his eyes wide, his mouth twisted into a silent scream.

◆ ◆ ◆

Rain was pelting the cabin's roof when they finally got the old woman off the floor and into a rocking chair near the fire. Wesley took her place on the floor and began inspecting the pile of parts that was once the Tin Woodsman.

The old woman seemed to be lost in her own little world. She had barely acknowledged their presence at all since tossing the Tin Man's severed head. Her eyes were vacant as she continued to mutter nonsense beneath her breath.

Hope knelt so she could look the strange woman in the eye. "What happened here? Why is the Tin Man in pieces?"

"Tin, tin. Little boy, bumps on his chin." The old woman looked over at Wesley and smiled a little black grin. Wesley had a screwdriver in one hand, but his other was already self-consciously fingering a small blemish just below his bottom lip.

Hope grabbed the woman's chin, forcefully shifting her attention back where it was supposed to be. "Pay attention!"

"Hey!" Taylor shouted. "Is that necessary?"

Hope ignored her. "We're looking for the young woman who lives with you. Where is she? Where did she go?"

The woman pulled away from Hope's harsh grip. She studied her for a long moment before the mischievous grin reappeared. She folded both hands in her lap and began to rock in her chair.

"Follow the yellow brick road!" She sounded like a kid who'd spent half her birthday hiding in a closet sucking air out of balloons. "Can't do that anymore, can we?"

"Do you know what happened?" Hope demanded. "It's like someone waved a wand and the whole thing just disappeared."

"Better find a new tune to sing! Ah!" Her shrill laughter returned. Taylor's skin crawled. She finally had to turn away, scrambling to join Wes on the floor.

She picked up one of the parts Wesley had brought over from the table. It was the Tin Man's left arm.

"His body's hollow," Wesley explained. "I'm surprised he doesn't blow away in the wind."

"Can you fix him?"

Wesley shrugged. "I don't know. The screws are stripped. Even if they weren't, the screw heads are weird. This one is shaped like a moon. This one's a star." Taylor took one of the screws and began to inspect it. "Without the right tools we don't have a chance."

Hope joined them. "We're not getting anything out of that hag."

"Don't call her that," Taylor said.

"Can you put him back together?"

"Not here," Wesley said. "Even if I do, that doesn't mean he'll be *alive.*" Taylor could tell Wesley didn't know if that was the right word.

"Great," Hope smirked. "That's just great! Alright, I promised to get you here, but if there's nothing you can do we need to go back. You two can wait in the library, and I'll get the amulet to The Librarian myself."

Taylor ignored her. "What about the tinsmith? The man who put the Tin Man together in the first place."

"You know," Wesley began, "that's not a bad idea."

"Now wait a minute–"

Taylor turned to the old woman who was pumping her feet in-and-out to make the chair rock. "Ma'am? Is there a town nearby? Someplace we might–"

"Wheelers and monkey wings. These are a few of my favorite things!"

Hope rolled her eyes and started for the door. "If I have to spend one more minute with this woman I'm going–"

"Wait!"

The woman's command came from deep inside and left them frozen in place. It wasn't the voice of a lost soul; it was the cry of a frightened woman with nowhere to go.

“Don't go!” she begged. “Please! I can't get on alone. I can't do this myself.”

The woman rose from her chair then slowly crept toward the children. Taylor stiffened as the old woman took the Tin Man's limb from her.

“You don't understand,” the woman explained. “I did this to him.” She held the cold metal to her wrinkled cheek. “I did this to *them*.” Wesley and Taylor exchanged a confused look. “He was a good boy. So nice, so respectful. I just couldn't be alone.” She looked at Taylor. “They took her, you know? They came, and they took her. That poor little girl.”

“Who?” Taylor asked.

The woman smiled like a rotten kid who'd just lured her baby sister into an elaborate trap. “Wheelers and monkey wings. Favorite things!”

Her grin grew, and Taylor saw she had teeth after all. Some were grey, others black and white. They looked like tiny headstones jutting out of the wet ground.

Wesley stepped toward the woman and gently took the metal arm from her and put it into a large burlap sack he'd found near the fireplace. "C'mon, Tay. Let's go."

They finished stuffing the Tin Man's pieces into the sack then joined Hope in the doorway. Hope left the cottage. Wesley disappeared into the darkness behind her.

"Little girl?"

Taylor turned.

"If you find them, tell them I'm sorry."

"I will," Taylor promised.

"If I'd known this would happen..."

The old woman didn't finish. She didn't have to.

"I know exactly what you mean."

Taylor nodded a polite goodbye to the old woman before moving through the doorway and into the night, quietly hoping the rain would wash away any tears that came... and the guilt that went along with them.

◆ ◆ ◆

Taylor stepped onto the porch where Wesley and Hope were waiting with the sack of Tin Man parts at their feet. She had to shield her eyes from the rain. They were standing beneath an overhang, but gusting winds were sending some of the rain their way.

Wesley slung the backpack from his shoulder and pulled his copy of *Oz* from its pouch. "I think there's a map in here." He flipped to the back. "Yeah. See?"

An illustrated map was spread across two pages near the back of the book. It was quite thorough, showing all the major features and landmarks within Oz.

Wesley pointed to the drawing of a small cottage. "It says this is the Tin Man's cabin. And look, there's a village pretty close to that." He slid his finger across the page and stopped near a few hand drawn buildings.

"How do we know that's the right one?" Hope asked.

"Why *wouldn't* he go to the nearest tinsmith?"

Taylor leaned forward so her nose was just inches from the page. "Look at that! Look what's happening to the yellow brick road!" There was a dashed line that cut through the drawing toward Emerald City in the center of Oz. The line was half gone and seemed to be disappearing a little at a time from the page.

"What's happening?"

"I don't know," Wesley answered.

"Great," Hope complained. "If the map's changing, how do we know we can trust it at all?"

Wesley slammed the book shut. "It's all we've got."

"You're right," Hope said. "Do we even have a *plan*?"

Taylor and Wes looked to one another. Hope shook her head with disgust.

"You know? You should really know what you're trying to do before you set off on a quest like this. Take the ring away from Frodo and all you've got is a bunch of guys with hairy feet walking around the forest together."

"We'll have a plan once we've put the Tin Man together. C'mon. We're wasting time." Taylor grabbed the sack and started down the steps.

"Are we really going to walk around in this rain?" Wesley had to speak up so he would be heard over the storm. "Maybe we should go back inside and wait this out. It's like a freakin' monsoon out here!"

Taylor turned. "We're leaving now."

"What?" Wesley asked. "Why?"

"Because the map's changing, Wes. This isn't over. Things might get even worse."

"She's right," Hope said. "You guys don't know what's waiting in these woods now that the sun's set. Let's go back to the library and–"

"No!" Taylor exclaimed. "We're not going back!"

Exasperated, Hope shook her head.

"Fine," Wesley said. "The rain won't be as bad once we're in the forest, anyway."

Taylor smiled at Wes then heaved the heavy bag of metal parts over her shoulder and started up the hill that had turned to a muddy, slippery mess in the rain.

Hope turned to Wesley. "She feels bad about all this, huh?"

"It's more than that," Wesley explained. "Things were bad for her when we got back. It's like her whole life got turned upside down."

"That doesn't mean she should be in charge, Wes. Do what you want, but I thought she would have learned to listen to you by now."

CHAPTER 9

THE WICKED WITCH of the West looked nothing like the actress who portrayed her in the movie. The real Witch was a frumpy woman. Her skin was green, but it was wrinkled and sagged away from her face. Her clothes were a wild mismatch of style and color. She wore a regal shirt with a ruffled collar and paired it with black pants embroidered with strange symbols. Her hair was braided in three messy ponytails that extended from beneath the tall pointed hat atop her head.

Randy watched the Witch lean on her umbrella as she approached them. If he had seen her in the real world – and she wasn't green – he would have assumed the Witch to be an old bag lady who'd lost her way. It was easy to imagine given her rumpled appearance. He wouldn't have feared her at all. In fact, he wouldn't have feared *this* version of the Witch if it weren't for her eye.

The Witch had but one good eye. Never blinking, it bulged from its socket so grotesquely that Randy couldn't understand why it hadn't popped from her skull and fallen to the floor. The red veined marble was constantly moving, taking everything in, no doubt looking for the one responsible for the black patch that covered the void where her other eye had been.

"You don't look like a sorcerer," the Witch began.

"I'm not," Douglas answered coolly.

"Ah! My guards tell me you are quite powerful." Her voice sent a shiver up Randy's spine. "Of course," she continued, "my guards are foolish and know little. I can never trust what they tell me."

As if on cue, one of the guards who had escorted them into the castle offered Douglas's pistol to the angry woman. She snatched it from his hand, snarling at him until he backed into the corner and looked away.

Douglas waited patiently as she studied the weapon.

"They say you used this noisemaker to kill my best man. They say its sound tore through his armor and left a gaping wound in his chest."

"It wasn't the sound – not exactly."

"Then what manner of magic *is* this?"

"We don't call it magic where I'm from," Douglas explained. "Most people don't believe in magic. Where I'm from we call it something else. We call it science."

Randy flinched when the Witch's eye looked up sharply at his father. "You're from beyond the Deadly Desert, then?"

"You could say that."

She moved her attention back to the gun in her hand. She turned the heavy weapon over and squeezed the pistol's wooden stock in her fist.

"Be careful," Douglas whispered.

Her long fingers found the trigger and instantly understood its purpose. She lifted her arm and leveled the gun at Douglas's chest.

"Dad!"

She pulled the trigger.

Randy breathed a quiet sigh of relief when the only sound that came from the gun was a hollow click. Douglas smiled as if he'd seen the exchange coming from a world away.

The Witch grunted in frustration and shoved the weapon toward him. Douglas waved it off.

"Keep it," he said. "Please. I brought it for you. You'll need a little outside help if you're ever going to conquer Oz the way you've dreamed."

The Witch came alive in a fit of shrill laughter. "Oh, my dear! You are a stranger to these lands. There isn't a corner of Oz that hasn't fallen under my rule." She gestured with a long arm toward a nearby window as if the view alone would back her grand declaration.

Douglas sighed. "You don't rule over anything, ma'am. Not even Winkie Country. I'm sorry, but it's true."

The guards in the corner shared a nervous look.

"You shouldn't say such things when I hold your only power in my hand."

"If it helps, the old man in Emerald City has never ruled either. Neither has Glinda the Good or the Gnome King or anyone else in Oz. This world's been ruled by one man since the very beginning, and he's never even been here."

Her mouth twisted into a snide question. "Who?" she asked. "Pray tell."

"His name is L. Frank Baum."

Randy saw the Witch react as if the author's name meant something to her. "And does he rule using magic like this?" She extended her hand to show the gun balanced on her deeply lined palm.

"He uses something far more powerful, I'm afraid. *His words*."

◆ ◆ ◆

Wesley, Taylor, and Hope stood on the outskirts of a small town where a strange message had been scrawled into the mud at their feet. The words were written in tall, uneven letters that had filled with rainwater and now reflected the moon's hazy light. While the greeting had eroded in part, it was still easily read: BeWare tHe WHeeLERS!

"What does *that* mean?" Hope asked.

Taylor shook her head without answering. Even the assistant librarian needed to take a class in Oz lore, it seemed.

The three of them continued down the muddy path that led into the tiny, one-street village. Their feet splashed in puddles as they surveyed the wreckage before them.

The entire town was in shambles. The night sky was alive with the orange glow of fire as a tiny church in the center of town burned. Doors were ripped from their hinges. The windows on storefronts were shattered. A wailing toddler was digging through boxes spilled from an overturned wagon in the street.

"What happened here?" Wesley asked.

"Did you expect something different?" Hope answered.

Taylor walked toward the crying child near the wagon. "Hey," she said softly. "You okay? You–"

The young boy ran to her, wrapping both arms around Taylor's waist and burying his sad face in her shirt.

"Whoa! Calm down," she said. "It's okay." Taylor knelt down to pick the boy up. "Can you tell me what happened?"

Side-by-side, Wesley and Hope continued deeper into town while Taylor lagged a few paces behind to make friends with the crying boy.

There were other children, too. A young girl with a dirty face was wandering aimlessly in front of the general store. A shirtless boy sat in the town's square with his legs crossed while two round faces pressed the glass of a second-story window looking like a pair of curious ghosts.

"Where is everyone?" Taylor asked.

Wesley pointed to a crooked sign labeled "Tinsmith" over a pair of swinging doors that led into a small corner building. "Let's hope he can help."

"Shouldn't we find this guy's parents?"

"We will, Tay! Jeez! First things first."

Taylor winced at Wesley's sharp tone.

Wesley stepped easily onto the porch outside the tinsmith's shop, its wood creaking beneath his feet. Taylor and Hope followed him inside. It was pitch black, nothing but a few fingers of moonlight reaching through the window to light the room.

"Hello?" Wesley asked. He stepped deeper into the shop. There were items on shelves available for sale: cake pans and pots, teakettles and utensils. A cluttered workbench was pressed against a wall behind the counter. There was an anvil with a large sledgehammer beside that. "Anyone here?"

All at once there was a clatter from behind the counter. Wes turned as long metal rods spilled onto the floor followed by a flash of blonde hair in the darkness.

"Wait!" Wesley yelled. "Grab her!"

A young girl rounded the counter and made a beeline for the exit. Hope moved into her path, grabbing her hand and wrenching it so hard the little girl came off her feet, her soot-covered face twisting in pain.

"Stop it!" Taylor screamed. "You're hurting her!"

"It's fine, Tay. Someone has to tell us what happened."

Wesley's cold tone was back. He seemed to be getting harder as their adventure progressed – if you could even call it an adventure this time around.

He approached the small girl. She tried to break away, but Hope tightened her grip.

"It's okay," Wesley explained. "We're not going to hurt you. Can you tell us what happened here? To your village? Were you attacked?" The girl didn't answer. "Do you know where we can find the tinsmith?" His mention of the metalworker brought a glimmer of recognition to the girl's pale blue eyes.

"Great," Hope huffed. "Another comatose patient."

"Enough!" Wesley snapped.

Tay grinned. It was nice to see him giving Hope the same attitude she'd been getting over the last few hours. Taylor was beginning to worry Wesley was mad at her. Seeing him snap at Hope eased her concerns, if only for a little bit.

Wesley fell to one knee and pulled a bottle of water from his backpack.

"You thirsty?"

The girl was reluctant but eventually took the bottle. She looked at it with curious eyes, swirling the water around inside the plastic container.

Wes laughed beneath his breath. "Let me." He offered his hand. The girl handed the bottle over then watched with great interest as Wesley unscrewed the cap and took a drink. She smiled, and Wesley handed her the bottle. She took a small sip. Then, as soon as her lips were wet, she tipped the bottle back and nearly swallowed its contents with a single gulp.

"Hit the spot?"

The girl nodded, and Wesley sat down in front of her.

"What's your name?"

The girl thought long and hard before answering.

"Nell."

"Nell? That's a pretty name," Wesley said. "Nell, can you tell me what happened? We're here to see the tinsmith. Is he—"

“No!” she hollered. “I don't want to talk about that!”

Nell stood up and marched to a dark corner where her brimming emotions would go unseen. “My pa is gone,” the strange girl whispered. “They're all gone. Nothin’ 'round here now but us kids.”

❖ ❖ ❖

Wesley and Hope sat on the counter as Taylor and the boy from outside watched their new friend work. Nell was standing on a small stool so she could use her father's workbench while trying to piece the Tin Man together again.

While the metalworker's tools looked awkward in her tiny hands, Nell made due. She had all the tools necessary along with new screws to replace those that had been stripped during the Tin Man's dismemberment. The Tin Man's metal torso was sitting upright on the bench and already had one arm attached.

“What if this doesn't work?” Wesley asked.

“What if it *does*?” Hope wondered aloud.

Nell reached for a three-handled wrench on a shelf above her head. It was just out of reach, and she nearly lost her balance, grabbing hold of the bench to keep from falling. When she did, the movement was just enough to rattle the Tin Man's torso. The arm she'd attached fell from its socket and landed on the bench with a hollow thud.

"Dang it," Wesley said.

Nell shuddered, her eyes fixed on the silver limb. She began to whimper. Taylor couldn't decide if the little girl was scared or sad. She suspected it was a little bit of both. *A lot* of both, actually.

"It's okay," Taylor said. "What can I do to help?"

Taylor picked up the arm, and the two began working together. With Tay there to assist, it didn't take Nell long. When finished, she stepped back to appraise her work. The Tin Man's arms were now firmly in place where they belonged.

His legs were ready to go, but Nell grabbed his head next, gently setting it in place on the Tin Man's shoulders. Once balanced, she grabbed her tool and began to tighten the screws that held his head in place. As soon as the first screw was threaded, the Tin Man came to life.

"PLEASE!" he shouted. *"NO! PLEASE! DON'T!"*

Nell pulled away, falling off the stool and onto her backside. The Tin Man's head swiveled back and forth frantically.

"TAKE ME! TAKE ME! I'LL KILL YOU—"

The screw rattled loose, and the head rolled off his shoulders and fell to the floor.

Nell turned to Taylor. "Please," she pleaded. "Don't make me do this! I can't look at him! I knew he'd come back to get me!"

"He isn't going to hurt you," Taylor said. "Why would you think that?" Taylor looked down at the Tin Man's head just as it spun to a stop in the corner. This time his frozen face seemed crooked, like it was about to slide off and reveal the mechanism lying beneath.

"He said he's gonna kill us!" Nell shouted.

"He wasn't talking to us."

"I told my pa! I told him the woodchopper would keep comin' back and when he was nothin' but tin he was gonna want to chop somethin' other than wood. I told him!"

Taylor forced a laugh, hoping it might comfort the young girl. "You don't have anything to worry about, Nell. He's our friend. He wouldn't hurt anyone."

"You promise?"

"He seems more scared than you. Don't you think?"

"I guess. What happened to him?"

"That's what we're here to find out."

Taylor bent at the waist and gently scooped the Tin Man's head into both hands. She was sure to turn his face away so Nell wouldn't see the nasty expression he was now wearing. "Here," she said. "I'll hold him in place. All you have to do is tighten the screws."

Nell bit nervously at her lip before offering an agreeable nod. She grabbed the screwdriver with a moon-shaped head and climbed back onto her stool. Her fingers trembled as she guided the first screw into place.

Just as he'd done before, the Tin Man began to scream as soon as the screw was home. *"LET HER GO! I SWEAR IF YOU HURT HER..."*

Nell jumped from the stool and put her back to the wall as the Tin Man began to assess his surroundings.

"What's going on? Where am I?!" His eyes fell on Taylor. "*You! You* did this!"

The Tin Man batted an arm at Taylor, and though he presented no real threat, Wes hopped off the counter and came between them.

"She *saved* you," Wesley said. "*That's* what she did."

The Tin Man looked Wesley in the eye then moved his gaze to Taylor and gave an apologetic nod. "I'm sorry, madam. It has been a trying time. Tell me, do you know what has become of my fiancée?"

"We were hoping you could tell us," Wesley said.

The Tin Man lowered his eyes. "I only know that they took her."

"Who?"

"I'm not for certain. We–"

A chilling screech from outside cut the Tin Man short.

"Umm... what was that?" Hope asked nervously.

"I don't know," Wesley explained. "I–"

The squeal occurred twice more. It sounded like an old radio dialing between frequencies, but Taylor couldn't help thinking there was something *alive* responsible for the painful cry.

Nell covered her ears with both hands. Another series of quick shrieks cut through the night.

Laughter followed, high pitched and manic, like something out of a nightmare.

"Hide!" Nell hollered. "Hurry! Hide!" She slid beneath the workbench and grabbed a pair of metal shears for protection.

The Tin Man lurched forward, tottered, then fell off the workbench and landed face first on the floor.

"My legs! Help me to attach my legs!"

Tay hustled over to help. "We will," she said. "Just–"

"NOW!"

Wesley grabbed one of the metal limbs from the table but fumbled as he tried to line the leg's ball-joint up with the socket in the Tin Man's torso. He looked to Nell for help, but she wasn't coming out from beneath the bench. She was ready to give anyone the business end of her shears if they tried to make her.

"I've got it," Taylor said. She grabbed the screwdriver and a pair of screws from the bench and went to work.

The psychotic laughter grew louder as it circled the shop. Every so often the laughs were punctuated with another ear-splitting squeal.

The Tin Man watched Wesley and Taylor finish with one leg before moving to the next. Both kept looking over at the shop's double doors, clearly worried the shrieking laughter would eventually make its way inside.

"Help me up," the Tin Man ordered. They did, letting the metal man lean on them until he was ready to stand on his own.

"Look," Hope said from a nearby window. "It's them."

"Who?" Taylor whispered.

"Remember? Beware the Wheelers."

Taylor looked out the window, making sure to stay hidden as best she could. At first, all she saw was the empty street. But then, something streaked into view and began turning circles in the town square.

While similar to humans in form, the Wheelers traveled on all-fours like a beast. Their arms and legs were equal in length with thin wheels at the end of each appendage instead of hands and feet. They wore colorfully embroidered clothing and straw caps perched on their heads.

Taylor watched the Wheeler roll to a halt before arching its back and letting out another of the painful shrieks. In the distance, another answered. Then, the frenzied laughter returned.

Taylor turned to Nell. "Don't worry, sweetheart. They can't do anything to us."

Hope furrowed her brow. "What are you talking about? Aren't these the ones the old woman was talking about?" She looked over at the Tin Man. "It's them, right? The ones who took your fiancée?"

He didn't answer.

"All the Wheelers can do is scare you," Taylor explained. "They have no hands to grab you with, no feet to kick. They aren't that bad at all, really. They're just... bullies. They can't do anything to you."

Wesley and Hope looked out the window again. A second Wheeler had joined the first. The two were circling the shirtless boy. One used his wheel to shovel dirt across the boy's face, laughing madly when the child began to cry.

"I don't know," Hope said. "They look pretty bad to me."

"We should help," Taylor suggested. She turned to find that the Tin Man was one step ahead of her, already pushing through the shop's wooden doors and dragging the tinsmith's heavy sledgehammer behind him.

Taylor and the others watched from the shop window as the Tin Man hobbled down the steps and into the street. The borrowed hammer left a trail in the mud behind him as he went. He reached the town's square unnoticed, his eyes alive with fury as they fell on the two Wheelers tormenting the young boy.

"That boy's done nothing to you!" the Tin Man boomed, his usually high voice sinking to a low and far-off place. "Leave him be!"

The Wheelers stopped, shifting their attention to the Tin Man. Confused, the first cocked his head to the side as if a new perspective might help him to understand. Unfazed, the second tossed his head back and shrieked. When the Tin Man didn't move one of the Wheelers began to giggle as he rolled toward him.

"yOu FReaK!" the Wheeler squealed. His voice sounded like tin foil. "bE gOnE, FooL! MEtAL mAn! LeaVE BeFORe wE TEaR yOU tO tINy, LitTlE BItS!"

He picked up speed, rolling past the Tin Man before circling around. But the Tin Man didn't budge. All he did was turn his head to watch as the Wheeler began skating in a tight circle around him.

"DoN'T yOU kNoW tHe WHEelERs, frEaK?! BeLIEve yOuR MEtAL eYeS! wE aRe NoT tO Be tRiFLeD wITh! wE KiLL wItHOuT tHiNKinG! wE'vE CoME FroM tHe LaND oF eV tO SWaLLoW yOuR sOuL!"

"I know who you are," the Tin Man whispered. "And now I know your secret."

"We HaVE nO SeCreTs!"

The Wheeler's laugh grew until his deafening cackle drowned out the night. He was so caught up that he didn't notice the Tin Man had raised the sledgehammer and was now gripping it tightly in both hands.

The Wheeler's friend squealed a warning, but it was too late. The Tin Man swung the hammer just as he'd swung his axe so many times before. It caught the Wheeler with such force that it knocked the wind from his lungs.

Suddenly silent, the Wheeler struggled to right himself. He'd fallen, and though he was born with them, he often found his wheels difficult to manage – especially when under duress.

The Tin Man buried the massive hammer in his chest again.

"Wes," Taylor cried. "We have to do something! He's gonna kill him!"

Wesley didn't respond, his wide eyes fixed on the action outside.

Taylor pushed by him in a huff and moved for the door. She could sense the Tin Man was about to go too far. She'd thought he went out to save the little boy. Instead, the Tin Man was looking for revenge. Something about that didn't feel right. Those kids were playing tug-o-war again, her heart pounding like it would break through her chest. It actually hurt. And why wouldn't it? The fight between right and wrong is often a painful one.

The Wheeler rolled onto his back. "PlEaSe," he cowered. "DoN't hURt mE! wE WeRe oNLy FUNniNG!" He held his long arms into the air, but they offered little protection. Just as Taylor explained, he had no hands to fight the Tin Man off, no feet to kick him away.

"How does it feel?" the Tin Man asked. "That helpless ache of despair?"

The Wheeler looked over at his friend. "HeLp mE, YoU DoLT!"

The Wheeler watching from the town's square let his head hang then turned to skate away.

"nO! sToP!"

"Maybe you should call your monkey friends. Maybe they can help you."

The Wheeler looked up at him. "PlEaSE," he cried. "TeLL mE wHaT yOu WaNt! i'LL dO aNyTHiNG!"

Taylor came out of the shop just in time to see the Tin Man raise his sledgehammer into the air. "No! *Don't!*"

But the Tin Man didn't listen. He brought the hammer down in one last violent arc and the Wheeler's shrieking came to an end.

CHAPTER 10

RANDY HAD SPENT most his life admiring his father. Douglas was his hero, his idol – the epitome of everything he wanted to be. But the shiny veneer was beginning to wear thin. People in Astoria had often described Douglas Stanford as a hard and ruthless man: someone who would do anything to get his way. Randy had always scoffed at the notion, but the evidence before him now was difficult to deny. He was finally seeing his father as others did. Douglas had done terrible things since stepping into Astoria's library, and while Randy could find a way to justify most of it, this was different. Douglas had taken an audience with the Wicked Witch of the West – one of the most feared villains of all time – and she was treating him as an equal.

Even worse, the two seemed to be becoming friends.

"You say all of Oz is controlled by this man in your world," the Witch said, repeating information Douglas had already conveyed. "Anything he writes in his book *there*... happens *here*?" Douglas nodded, smiling until she batted him away with her hand. "Then he's already given me everything I want," the Witch said. "Why do I need you?"

Randy saw Douglas frown. He knew the Witch wasn't supposed to rule in Oz, but if he understood his father correctly, Wesley and Taylor had altered the Oz story in their visit. Now his dad was in a tough spot. How was he supposed to deal with the Witch if she didn't think she needed any help?

"You have what you want," Douglas said. "*For now.* But you don't know how the book ends. Baum wrote fourteen books about Oz. You know how many he put you in?" The Witch watched Douglas raise a single finger. "If your rule of this land's to last, don't you think you'd exist beyond the first book?"

"Bah! Who's heard of such things? Books that come true? I'll take my chances before shaking hands with some outlander in strange clothes that's come to me with such tall tales."

Douglas stepped toward her. "You're skeptical. I understand. I do. I'm a stranger in your land, and you have no reason to trust me. Not one. But what if you're wrong? If you listen to me and I'm wrong, you've lost nothing. But if you ignore me and I'm *right...*"

Her bulging eye went to the pistol sitting on a stone table nearby. "You can grant me this power?" she asked with a nod toward the gun.

"I can arm every one of your guards with a noisemaker like this one. And there's more where that came from. My world is home to weapons you can't imagine. Bigger. Louder. You'll have access to as many as you need. Your rule in Oz will never end. I guarantee it."

Her expression gave nothing away. Until, finally–

"Fine," she said. "What is it you want from me?"

❖ ❖ ❖

Everyone sat in a circle around a fire the village children had built for the group to stay warm. Nearly a dozen pale kids had come out of hiding. They'd scavenged for food in the general store then nestled in with Taylor and Wesley to hear the Tin Man's tale – a story that began just after his heartfelt reunion with his fiancée, the Munchkin maiden.

"We left shortly after the two of you went home," the Tin Man told Taylor and Wes. "We were ready to put all of Oz between us and that dreadful woman in the woods." He looked into the darkness beyond. "We hoped to get as far as we could before sunset, but the sky turned black long before it rightly should. Storm clouds rolled in from the horizon. Lightning flashed. Thunder rolled. It was unlike any storm I'd ever seen. Flowers at our feet began to wilt. Plants withered before our eyes. Then... it was so strange... it was like... the end days. Everything around us began to fade. The whole world turned the color of ash."

His voice wavered as he continued. "The earth began to quake beneath us. I couldn't stay on my feet." He looked at Nell in Taylor's lap. "Your father did a fine job building this metal body, but my balance is nothing like it once was." His words quickened. "I told my fiancée to leave me behind, but she wouldn't. We started back for the cabin. We had to get out of the storm, even if it meant confronting the old woman again. I fell a dozen times along the way, but my love was always there to pick me up." He hung his head. "She was there to catch me every time."

"How long did the quake last?" Hope asked.

"Not long. It was over by the time we arrived. We found the old woman hiding beneath her bed." Thoughts of the old woman cowering brought a grin to the Tin Man's face, but it quickly faded. "The rains came next. It washed the grey away, and for a brief moment, I thought things would go back to the way they were, that the darkness would pass."

"Is that when they came?"

"The Wheelers?" the Tin Man asked. "I'd heard of them, of course. They terrorize all who live in the Land of Ev, but I've never known them to be in Oz." He shook his head. "They kept circling the house. Those noises they make. And the laughing. That *awful* laughing. It was more than I could take. It was raining, but I unlocked the door and stepped onto the porch with my axe. I was hoping to scare them away, but the monkeys... they were waiting... they were working together, you see? And I... I was so foolish. The Wheelers *made* me open the door."

Wesley's mind drifted back to the old woman and her strange chant. *Wheelers and monkey wings*, she'd said. *These are a few of my favorite things*. It had been the ramblings of a mad woman. Then. Now? Now it made a lot more sense.

"The monkeys pulled me into the cabin. The old woman was screaming from under the bed. And those Wheelers... they just kept laughing." The Tin Man closed his eyes. An oily teardrop fell down his cheek. "The monkeys held me down and pulled my love into the doorway. Then... they... they made her watch."

"What do you mean?" Wesley asked.

"They didn't take her away until they were done with me. They held her there, in the doorway." He tried to wipe his tears away, and his joints screamed for oil. "I couldn't stop them. There were too many. I *swear* I tried, but... they ripped off my arms. Then my legs. Then..." More black tears began to roll.

A long silence fell over them when the Tin Man was finished. His weren't the only tears. Many of the children were crying, too.

"I'm sorry," Taylor said.

"Why would you apologize?" the Tin Man asked.

"Because we–"

"She's sorry for *your loss*," Hope interjected. "We *all* are."

The Tin Man studied Taylor before giving an appreciative nod that made his joints squeak. Taylor stood up and took the oil can from a sack nearby so she could oil his joints.

Wesley ran a hand through his hair and blew out a deep breath. "What if we told you we could help make things go back to the way they were?"

This time the Tin Man's cold gaze fell on the boy. "You returned because you knew this would happen, I think." Wes looked away beneath his icy stare. "I knew you were different," the Tin Man continued. "You aren't from Oz or any of her lands."

No one spoke.

Then–

"You're right," Taylor whispered.

"Taylor!" Hope exclaimed.

"He already knows!" Taylor turned to face the Tin Man. "You're right. We're from another world. One far away from here."

Hope shot Wesley a look. "See?! This is why *you* should be talking!"

Taylor ignored them. “We're here to help, but we can't fix things in Oz without you.”

“How can we help?” the Tin Man asked.

Wesley grimaced. Yet again, someone was looking for answers they didn't have. It was his idea to come looking for the Tin Man and the Munchkin maiden, but who knew what they were supposed to do once they–

“We have to kill the Wicked Witch,” Taylor answered matter-of-factly.

“Gah! Do you know how many have died storming the Witch's castle?” the Tin Man asked in disbelief. “They've tried. But still, she lives.”

“That's because we're the only ones who can do it,” Taylor explained. “You, me... and two others.”

Wes wanted to argue, but couldn't. It was news to him, but there was poetic justice in Taylor's plan. While there had been small changes to the *Oz* book in the chapters immediately following the Tin Man's rescue, it wasn't until Dorothy's death that the story had jumped the tracks for good. If they were going to make this right – if it was even possible – it only made sense that they team with Dorothy's companions and return to the spot where she fell. And then, of course, someone would have to take Dorothy's place.

Wesley watched Taylor stand up and walk over to the Tin Man. "It isn't fair, I know. But it has to be us. No one else can do it." She looked over at Wesley. "And no one else can come."

"Who are these others you speak of?"

Taylor sighed. "A Scarecrow and a... a Cowardly Lion."

"A Cowardly Lion? Who's heard of such a thing? We'll never succeed!"

Taylor didn't respond. The Tin Man looked into the fire for answers.

"I'm sorry," he said. "I can't."

"What?" Wesley asked, sounding a bit stunned.

The Tin Man grabbed the sledgehammer and began to walk away. "Oz cursed me with this body then left me frozen in the forest so my love could be a slave to that awful woman in the woods. Why should I do anything for her?"

Taylor followed him. "But it was the Witch who cursed your axe. What if Oz did those things for a reason? What if Oz was preparing you for the battle to come?"

"Then she picked the wrong man." Taylor stopped as the Tin Man continued down the street that led out of town. "I'm sorry, but I won't lose her again. I wish I could help you. You helped me once. I owe you a debt for that. But she was there when I fell, I have to do the same for her: I have to find her."

Taylor watched him go, her mouth hanging open as she searched for any words that might give him pause. Anything that might keep him from leaving them forever. "I... I..."

Silent since the Wheelers' return, Nell suddenly yelled out after him. "Can I come?" The Tin Man looked back over his shoulder. "They took my pa," Nell explained. She was still holding the metal shears she'd taken from her father's shop. "That's where you're going, right? To save everyone the monkeys took? I want to come."

"Me too," the shirtless boy echoed.

"And me," another added.

Wesley watched as the children came to their feet one at a time. He could see The Tin Man didn't want any of them to join him, but he knew this was their only chance to save Oz, their only chance to fix things back home.

"There's too many to face on your own," Wesley explained. "You said it yourself."

The Tin Man turned to look Taylor in the eye. "I'm staying with the maiden once we find her. I won't go with you to kill the Witch."

Taylor nodded. "That's fine," she said. "If I can't do anything else, I want to get you back to the woman you love."

CHAPTER 11

THE LIBRARIAN FOLLOWED the trail along the canyon's edge until it ended near the sagging bridge. The Witch's castle was barely visible through the haze, but the old man could almost hear it taunting him, daring him to cross...

The bridge only looks *to be eons old*, it said.

You'll be safe...

Until you reach the other side.

He stepped onto the first wooden plank, testing its stability beneath his weight. The temperature had warmed somewhat, causing the canyon's mist to cover the bridge in a thin layer of condensation before it rose to mask the castle above. Although he was careful, The Librarian slipped, his foot shooting through the gap between two of the wooden planks. He recovered quickly, grabbing onto the bridge with his free hand but nearly losing his staff in the process.

The Librarian sighed. "Not as young as you were the last time, old boy. You're going to need this." He tightened his grip – one hand on the staff, one on the bridge's rope banister as he pulled himself back to his feet.

He cast a nervous glance back the way he'd come and considered finding another route. But he knew this was the only way. This was the same bridge Little Douglas Stanford had taken. He would do the same. He only hoped there was some remnant of the boy he once knew in the man Douglas had become. It was probably his only hope, and the fate of every known world was hanging in the balance.

❖ ❖ ❖

"Okay!" Taylor shouted. "All together! *Pull!*"

The Tin Man's joints whined as he heaved on a rope tied to the overturned wagon in the town's square. A dozen boys worked with him. Each had a rope of his own, and all were red-in-the-face as they pulled.

At first, it didn't look like the wagon would budge. But then, it slowly began to rise out of the mud. Once it was teetering on edge, momentum took over and the wagon fell back onto its wheels where it belonged.

Taylor applauded. “You guys rock!”

A few kids had been pulling so hard they fell backwards into the mud when the wagon finally gave way. They looked at one another and laughed, their worries briefly forgotten in their moment of success.

Wesley watched Taylor go to help them up and smiled. Even he could appreciate the moment of levity as he and Hope walked toward the general store to collect supplies.

“Wes,” Hope began, “why are you letting this happen?”

“What do you mean?”

“Why are we going with the Tin Man?”

“Taylor wants to help him find the Munchkin maiden.”

“I know that much. Why are we listening? This whole mess started because you brought those two together. Now we're gonna do it all over again? We don't even know where we're going? Taylor's gonna put these kids in danger so she can feel good about herself.” Hope pointed to the kids in the square.

"That's bull! They wanna go. So would I. So would *you*." Wesley led her through the doorway into the store. "And stop talking about Tay like that. You don't know her."

"But I *heard* her. *She* has to kill the Witch. Really? Since when? She's acting like you aren't even here."

"Do you have a better plan?"

"What happens if we run across someone who decides they want that pretty necklace hanging around your neck?" Hope shook her head. "I can't say much, Wesley, but I think The Librarian has plans for you."

"What do you mean?"

"He wouldn't have given you the amulet, otherwise. But he gave it to you because he thought you would protect it. The longer we're playing Kumbaya – it's at risk. Do I need to remind you it's our only way home?"

Wesley looked down at the metal bookmark that was draped over his chest then tucked it safely beneath his shirt.

"Tay always knows the right thing to do."

Hope ducked behind the store's counter and found a wicker basket to fill with food. "Says who? *Tay*? I've known girls like Taylor, Wes. I like her –

really, I do – but she wants all the glory." She started down one of the aisles. "You're here to save Oz, Taylor's here to play hero."

Wesley shook his head in frustration when she dipped around the corner.

He moved his gaze to the window. Outside, the kids were laughing. Taylor was right in the middle of the action – smiling and playing in the street like she didn't have a care in the world. Initially, Wes thought Taylor was only working to lighten their mood. The village kids had been through so much. But then, a young boy in the group patted Taylor on the back and it was *her* smile that grew. Another boy wrapped his arms around her. Taylor threw her head back and laughed. It was loud and boisterous. In all the time he'd known her, Wesley had never heard Taylor laugh like that before.

He looked down the aisle after Hope and frowned. He didn't know if Taylor was out for all the glory like Hope said, but she was definitely getting it.

◆ ◆ ◆

It was impossible to sneak up on the Witch's castle once atop the stone staircase. There was nothing to hide behind that might allow for a stealthy approach so The Librarian disguised himself as best he could. He walked with a hunch, dragging one leg and leaning on his staff as a feeble man might rely on a cane.

This time, there were ten guards outside the castle's gate, all of them on high alert. “Get back!” one of them yelled, stepping forward.

“Oh!” The Librarian called. “Don't worry your pretty, little heads about me.” He made sure his speech was slow and labored, just another piece of the persona he was hiding behind. “I'm only here to pitch my wares. I'll be on my way, but I have a great many deals for you and your men.”

“Does this look like a market to you? Go on! Git!” The guard pushed him away. The Librarian used his staff to stay on his feet.

“But I have something for everyone! Even you,” The Librarian insisted. He began to shuffle through his satchel. “Look here! You'll see!”

The guard looked back at the others and shrugged with amusement. When he turned to face the old man once more he saw The Librarian had removed a glass bottle with an orange liquid sloshing around inside.

"See? Rub this on your joints, and they'll never ache."

This earned the attention of a few more guards. They stepped forward. One of them cracked his neck to suggest he had good use for what the peculiar man was peddling.

The Librarian dropped the bottle into his satchel and removed a purple pouch tied with golden ribbon. "Mix this powder in your drink and you'll have the strength of ten men the next time you ride into battle."

"Hey," one of the men said. "We could use that!"

The Librarian watched with satisfaction as they drew closer. The guards were standing in a circle around him now, each waiting to hear more about the magic in the old man's bag.

"And this?" He drew his hand from the satchel one last time. This time there was no bottle or pouch, only a pile of grey powder sitting in the palm of his hand. "This one will make you wish you never sided with a creature as villainous as the Wicked Witch of the West."

The guards exchanged confused looks.

"Huh?"

"What do you—"

The Librarian blew the powder from his palm into the closest guard's face. The guard screamed, jabbing fat fingers into his eyes in a desperate attempt to get the powder out.

The Librarian tossed the remaining powder to the ground. Then, just as the guards were fumbling to pull swords from their scabbards, The Librarian slammed the end of his staff into the earth. *"Fumus!"*

The yellow stone atop his staff began to glow as the command echoed through the canyon below. Now armed, the guards looked down as the grey powder at their feet turned to a black cloud of smoke.

"Witch!" someone hollered. *"Witch!"*

The cloud enveloped them in an instant.

They were fighting blind.

"Fulgur!" The Librarian's command ignited the cloud with yellow lightning and several guards fell to the ground, writhing in pain.

The old man used his staff to disarm an attacking guard then swung it in a wide arc that cracked another across his jaw as he backed out of the cloud. *"Conturbo!"*

He turned and started for the castle. Behind him, still blinded by smoke, the remaining guards fought only each other.

"He's there!" one yelled.

"Grab him! Grab him!"

"That's me, you idiot!"

The guards were swinging their swords and reaching for shadows, completely unaware The Librarian had slipped away and was now charging for the–

An arrow cut through the air, whistling past The Librarian's head. Never slowing, he looked up, searching for the arrow's origin. There was an archer in the castle's watchtower. He was already pulling a second arrow from his quiver.

The old man pushed forward, desperate to reach the gate before the guard above had a chance to take aim. He stomped across the drawbridge, stretching his legs in long strides until–

The second arrow didn't miss. It caught The Librarian in his shoulder and spun him like a top before he fell to the ground in a heap of old bones just outside the castle's entry. He'd been so close that when his blood spilled, most of it flowed in a stream down the path and puddled on the tile just inside the castle's gate.

CHAPTER 12

THEY LEFT SHORTLY after sun-up. The village children piled into the buggy after loading it with food and supplies from the town's store. Wesley and Hope joined them in the back while Taylor sat in silence with the Tin Man as he guided the horse from the wagon's rumble seat.

The roads were treacherous. On more than one occasion, everyone had to climb out of the wagon to tighten a wobbly wheel or to fix a broken axle or because they had sunk so deeply into the mud that the horse needed help pulling the wagon out.

Even when the riding was smooth, it wasn't. The wagon's bumpy ride and rigid seats were a terrible combination. While the kids from the village seemed fine, Taylor thought the trip would beat her to death. The sun was just setting, but it felt like they'd been on the trail for days. Time seemed to have a life of its own in Oz. There were times when the hours seemed to crawl by, but just as often, they would sprint past in a flash. Tay had no idea how much time had passed since their return. The sun had risen twice and fallen for a third time, but that made little sense. They hadn't slept since stepping through the library's portal and had eaten little. They could never last three days without rest and food in the real world. Surely, they couldn't in Oz either. *Could they?*

◆ ◆ ◆

They rode through the night.

◆ ◆ ◆

The Tin Man stopped the wagon several hours after the moon made its first appearance. Their path was blocked by a number of tall trees that had been uprooted by some unseen force.

He and Taylor climbed out of the wagon to investigate and saw someone had cut another path through the forest that intersected their own. Trees were trashed and tossed to the wayside for as far as they could see in both directions.

The trees that survived the assault wept.

"What happened?" Taylor asked, directing her question to a tearful tree still standing near the road. "Who did this?" She wasn't sure why, but Taylor was convinced the wispy willow tree was a female.

"Those awful Gnomes," the willow said between sobs. "They did this. My poor girls. Look at them." She gestured toward the fallen trees with one of her delicate branches. "I suppose they couldn't be bothered to circle *around* our forest with that dreadful machine. No! They had to cut a path right *through* us."

"What machine?" the Tin Man asked.

"I don't know what it is," the willow said angrily. "How can you expect me to understand such evil? What is going on out there? Please, you must tell us. We've heard such terrible things. Have the end days come?"

Taylor let her head hang as the Tin Man answered.

"I wish I knew, ma'am."

The tree tried to contain herself. "You might as well cut me down, woodchopper. Without my girls, I... I..."

She began to cry again. Taylor and the Tin Man offered a few words of consolation then climbed back into the wagon and turned to go the other way.

◆ ◆ ◆

Time passed.

Eventually the Tin Man came across a tiny town in Munchkin Country where the men and women were preparing for a journey of their own.

"Where are you headed?" the Tin Man asked.

"Haven't you heard?" a Munchkin with rosy cheeks answered. "The Gnome King has come to grind down the road of yellow bricks. If that's true, we aren't going to wait around to see what happens."

He pointed down the yellow brick road. It wound through the meadow and passed right through their small village.

"It's all *her* fault, you know?" Taylor turned to face him, fearing this Munchkin knew more than the rest. "A girl very much like you dropped a house on the Witch's sister. That's when all of this began. There's a natural order to our world. That little girl changed things. I swear... if I ever see her again... she'll pay for what she's done."

"Things will get better," Taylor declared.

"Are you sure?" the Munchkin asked. "No one knows what's going to happen. How can you be sure of *anything* these days?"

Taylor didn't answer, and the Tin Man prodded the horse along.

◆ ◆ ◆

They were able to cover ground quickly once they were traveling on the solid path provided by the yellow brick road.

Just before dawn, disturbing screams echoed out to the travelers from just beyond the horizon. It was a horrifying sound, but they rode on. A few hours later, the Tin Man pulled on the horse's reins, stopping the wagon when he saw the road descend into a meadow at the base of a small hill.

Wesley and Hope hopped out of the wagon.

"What? Stuck again?" Hope asked snidely.

Neither Taylor nor the Tin Man turned to answer.

"Guys?" Hope prodded. "Hello?"

Taylor couldn't take her eyes from the scene in the distance. Neither could the Tin Man. Finally, Wesley and Hope followed their silent stare into the meadow below.

More than a dozen Gnomes were supervising a crowd of slaves straining to pry yellow bricks from the earth before tossing them into a colossal machine nearby. The machine was a mess of turning gears and thrusting pistons that belched steam through a bent exhaust pipe. It sat on wheels, and there was a loud grinding noise whenever the slaves threw a brick into its wide mouth. Once its sharp teeth were finished, the machine spat a stream of gold into a wagon that trailed behind it. A mountain of yellow dust sat piled in the wagon. Thousands of bricks, pulverized.

“My god,” Wesley said beneath his breath.

The Gnomes were strange beings made of stone. Their bodies were shaped like the jagged face of a mountain. Each was armed with a long whip. The whips cracked whenever someone stopped to rest or slipped on the uneven terrain. The lash was usually punctuated by an agonizing scream as one of the slaves hurried back to work.

The Tin Man watched intently as a winged monkey flew into sight with a new captive in hand. The monkey swooped low to the ground and dropped the young woman before arcing skyward and disappearing into the clouds.

The poor girl landed hard and tumbled to a stop near one of the Gnome's feet. The Gnome wasted no time. He yanked the girl up by the arm then shoved her toward the other slaves. She immediately fell to her knees and went to work loosening the next brick. The Gnome hadn't said a word. He didn't have to.

The Tin Man scanned every face trying to find the Munchkin maiden.

“Do you see her?” Taylor asked.

“She's there. I can feel it.”

Taylor gave a half-hearted smile.

“I *do* see your friends.”

“What friends?”

“Weren't you looking for a scarecrow and a lion?”

Taylor snapped her head around to look. Wesley rushed to her side. Sure enough, the Cowardly Lion was shackled with a leather harness attached to the Gnomes' machine. He was being whipped whenever the Gnomes needed him to inch the monstrosity along. Not as useful to them, the Scarecrow was bound to the machine's face like a hood ornament.

Wes couldn't believe it. "What are the chances we'd find them here?"

"You're lucky," Hope said.

Wesley wasn't so sure. Nothing about their journey had felt lucky.

Tay looked up at the Tin Man. "You have to help us free them, too. You don't understand. I'll–"

"I told you I was only here for my fiancée." He moved his sad eyes into the valley. "But you're right," the Tin Man continued. "We can't leave them like this." He raised his hammer. "We're going to save them all."

CHAPTER 13

A LITTLE AT a time, the Munchkin maiden made her way toward the new girl as a Gnome hurried over to shackle her feet and cuff her hands. With her head down, the maiden couldn't miss the polka dot pattern of fresh tears that had fallen into the golden dust at the new girl's feet.

The maiden waited until the Gnome was gone then got close enough to gently touch the girl's hand. "Don't be afraid," she whispered. "I'll help you."

The new girl wiped her tears, and the maiden quietly showed her what was expected. They worked together, using small tools to dig two yellow bricks up from the dirt before carrying them to the great machine and tossing them inside. They watched as the machine convulsed, grinding the bricks into powder.

An angry Gnome approached them. "Get moving, girls!"

The new girl hurried away, but the maiden grabbed her hand. “Go slow,” she explained. “That's the trick. If you tire yourself out, they'll whip you when you stop to rest.” She leaned in to whisper something in the new girl's ear. “Besides, you'll want your strength when it's time to escape.”

The maiden knelt down beside the road and grabbed a small pickaxe. She used it to dig at the next brick, but when she saw no one was watching she started to hammer away on the chains at her feet.

The new girl grinned. She'd definitely made the right friend.

“I've got news for you,” a man beside them said. “I've worked with metals my whole life. You aren't going to break these chains.”

“You aren't even going to try?” the maiden asked.

“Do you remember what happened to the old man they caught?”

The maiden looked over at the machine and shuddered. The new girl followed her gaze. She hadn't noticed before, but upon closer inspection she saw there was dried blood on the swirling teeth of the great machine. Someone had been ground down just like the bricks they were prying from the earth.

"That's probably what they'll do to all of us once were finished," the maiden suggested.

The man sighed. "We'll never be done, miss. This road goes on for miles in both directions. If we live to see it finished, I'm sure the Gnomes will just take us back into the mountains with them to work in their mines. The Gnome King won't stop until he's secured every precious metal and jewel in Oz. These truly are the end days."

The maiden shook her head. "I used to think such things. But miracles happen when we least expect them. When we've given up. That's why they're called miracles, after all." She looked into the distance. "Besides, I *have* to escape."

"Don't we all," he added.

"It's not the same. I have someone to get back to."

"Don't you think I'd like to see my little girl?"

The maiden sighed. "I wasn't trying to make little of your pain. But if I don't escape, who's going to put my fiancé back together again?"

Even the new girl reacted to the strange statement, looking up at the maiden in confusion.

"What happened to your fiancé?" the man asked.

"The monkeys ripped him apart when they took me. It was terrible. They ripped him limb from limb. Don't you see? I *have* to get back."

The man was careful with the words that came. "Sweetheart, you don't want to go back. Your fiancé... they killed him... you won't be able to put him back together again."

The maiden smiled. She'd forgotten to share her fiancé's *peculiar* condition. "Oh," she said. "I must sound crazy. No, you don't understand. I *can* put my love back together again. You see, my fiancé, he's... well... he's made of tin."

With that, she went back to work, hammering away on bricks, occasionally missing on purpose so that her hammer's head struck the chains on her feet. She'd completely missed the spark of recognition in the man's eye. He knew her fiancé, you see. He'd built him. He was the tinsmith. He was Nell's father.

❖ ❖ ❖

"I can't believe I'm doing this," Hope mumbled. She looked down her nose at Taylor and Wes from atop the wagon. She was in the driver's seat but wasn't happy to be there.

"You'll be fine," Taylor explained.

"Yeah," Wesley said. "Trust me."

"I can't believe this was *your* idea! You're supposed to be the smart–"

Wesley smacked the horse before he had to hear any more. It took off, galloping wildly down the road with the wagon. Hope nearly fell out of her seat as the wagon bucked beneath her.

"Wes!" Taylor exclaimed.

"Like you weren't thinking the exact same thing!"

The kids watched the wagon descend the hill. Wesley was laughing until he looked over and saw Taylor was too. He leveled cold eyes at her and smirked.

"What?" she asked.

He started for the woods. "C'mon. Let's go."

Taylor looked confused as she went after him.

"Hey!" she said. "You were laughing, too!"

◆ ◆ ◆

Hope gained control of the wagon just as it rolled to a silent stop within sight of the Gnomes. Too busy to notice the intrusion, the Gnomes and the slaves were completely unaware of her presence. Hope had no idea what she was supposed to say and blurted the first thing that came to mind.

"What's going on here?"

The Gnomes looked up in unison. Their block faces showed no expression as they stared at the unexpected intruder. They were repulsive creatures and reminded Hope of the ugly sculptures first graders sometimes bring home from art class.

"Get her!" one of them finally yelled.

The slaves stopped to watch as three Gnomes marched toward her. Hope jumped from her seat, hopping down from the wagon and stumbling just a bit as she began to run away.

They pursued her up the hill, but the Gnomes were awkward creatures with stubby legs. They had little chance of catching her until one flicked his whip and caught Hope's ankle, pulling her to the ground.

Hope scrambled to get up, but whenever she was about to right herself the Gnome would yank on his whip and she'd fall again. He laughed. They all did. They had her surrounded in no time.

"Get to your feet, woman! You have work to do!"

Hope rolled onto her back. She looked up at her captors. A crooked grin crept onto her face. The very idea that she dared smile infuriated the Gnomes even further.

"Do I look like I'm joking, outsider?"

One of them pulled Hope to her feet then shoved her down the hill. But his anger quickly turned to alarm when he saw what was waiting.

All of the village children had piled out of the wagon's buggy to confront the Gnomes. The Tin Man was there, too - front and center. And while the kids weren't that intimidating - even with the tools they held like weapons - all three Gnomes saw there was blood on the hammer in the Tin Man's hands. He had already done some damage and looked eager to do some more.

Hope's smile grew as she looked back at the Gnomes. "Did I forget to tell you about my friends?"

Without thinking, the other Gnomes ran to help and left the slaves unattended near the monstrous machine. One of them looked back and barked an order. "Keep working, you! This won't take–"

The Tin Man bashed the Gnome with his hammer before he could finish. Several children threw themselves on top of him and did their best to pin him. When he finally came to his feet again, the Gnome had a skinny boy on his back and a little girl wrapped around one of his legs. He was no match for the nimble children. They held tight as he swatted and shrugged, clumsily trying to shake free from their grip.

That was how much of the battle progressed. The Tin Man would send a Gnome crashing to Earth with his hammer, and the kids would pounce on top to keep him there. They weren't winning, exactly. The Tin Man's rage-powered hammer wasn't enough to hurt the Gnomes, and the village children were a nuisance more than anything else. But they were slowing them down. And distracting them.

The plan had worked to perfection.

Taylor and Wes snuck from the woods and darted through the meadow toward the slaves. Making sure to go unseen, Wesley slid through the grass and hid behind the machine while Taylor hurried to free the Scarecrow.

"Who are you?" The straw man's voice was scratchy and weak.

"Shh! We're friends."

"You should go. If the Gnomes find you–"

"It's fine," Taylor whispered. "We're here to help."

Wesley poked his head out just in time to see the Tin Man take another Gnome down.

The Cowardly Lion was nearby, hiding beneath giant paws and trembling. "W-w-what's h-happening?"

"Where are the keys?" Wesley asked.

Without looking, the Lion pointed toward a ring of brass keys hanging from a hook nailed to the machine. Wesley grabbed it and started toward the slaves.

Nell's father shuffled over to greet Wes. "What's going on? Who are you?" His shackles jangled as he moved to get closer.

"Are you the tinsmith?"

"Yes, but–"

"I'm friends with your daughter. We're here to rescue you."

"You *know* Nell?"

Wesley started to answer, but the tinsmith cut him off.

"What do you mean *we're* here to rescue you?"

Most of the slaves were watching the action unfold just fifty yards away. Although the wagon obstructed much of their view, some were starting to recognize the children.

"Is that... that's *my boy!*"

"Those are *our* kids!"

"What?!"

Nell's father wheeled around to look with the others.

"What is my daughter doing here?" one of them yelled.

"That's Eli!" someone screamed.

"Is she here?" the tinsmith asked angrily. "Did you bring my Nell with you?!"

"I... I..."

"Unlock me! *Now!*"

Wesley fumbled with the keys. He was desperate to find the right one, but his hands were seizing up with fear. Finally, after several failed attempts, one of the keys slid home into the shackles that bound the tinsmith's feet. He turned the key, and the shackles popped open with a soft click. A moment later, Wesley'd done the same with the cuffs on the big man's wrists.

"You shouldn't have done this," the tinsmith said.

He started to leave, but Wesley stopped him with an outstretched hand.

"Wait! You have to help! Please!"

"But Nell–"

"We have to free the others before it's too late."

Seeing the tinsmith free filled the others with a sense of excitement and desperation. They pushed between Wesley and the tinsmith and anxiously shoved their cuffed hands into Wesley's face.

"Please, child!"

"Help!"

"I have to save my son!"

"The key! Give us the key!"

It overwhelmed Wesley to see so many faces looking to him as their only hope. His hands began to shake under the pressure. He had the right key, but now he couldn't fit it through the keyhole.

Once Taylor and the Scarecrow had freed the Lion of his massive harness, Tay pushed through the crowd and came to Wesley's side. The Munchkin maiden recognized her immediately.

"It's *you! Again!*"

Taylor nodded a quick affirmation but didn't take time for more. She was there to help Wes. "Calm down," she said. "One at a time. Give him room, guys."

But the mob was growing impatient. Their dirty hands grabbed at the keys. One of the slaves yanked Wesley by the arm. Another pulled him in the opposite direction.

"Stop!" the maiden screamed. *"They're here to help!"*

It looked like the crowd might turn on Wes and tear him to pieces. They were desperate. Desperate for freedom. Desperate to save their kids.

Nell's father was about to leave. He took a few steps toward the wagon, ready to find Nell and escape. Instead, he stepped in and put his broad-shouldered body between Wesley and the other slaves.

"Stop it! This is our only chance! Do you want to see our kids enslaved, too?"

As that grim possibility sank in, the slaves finally backed off and gave Wesley room to work. Each waited their turn, but it was a struggle for all. Their children were *so* close. And they were no longer screaming joyfully as they engaged the Gnomes, many were now crying in pain as the skirmish took its toll.

Finally, one of the slaves couldn't take it any more. As soon as his cuffs were off, he sprinted to join the fight.

"No!" the tinsmith said. *"Wait!"*

But it was too late. The man was already screaming his son's name. "Eli! *Eli!*"

The Gnomes turned. Horror filled their sunken eyes when they saw they'd been duped and their slaves were now free.

"No! The King's slaves! Don't let them get away!"

The slaves ran for their children; children ran for their parents. Meanwhile, the Tin Man kept swinging wildly, using his hammer to slow any Gnomes within reach.

"Run!" the Tin Man yelled. *"Run, children! Run!"*

Taylor waited for Wes to free the last of the adults then grabbed his hand.

"The woods!" Taylor screamed. *"Go into the woods!"*

Taylor and Wes sprinted for the tree line together. All around them adults pushed their children to do the same as the Gnomes closed in.

Just a moment before, the kids had been the saviors – but now the parents were free and everyone seemed to be falling into their natural roles.

"This way," Taylor said.

Taylor led Wesley down a dirt path that cut through the forest. The villagers stayed in a group, doing their best to evade the Gnomes together. Only one of the Gnomes broke away to follow Taylor and Wes. The rest pursued the main group as they disappeared into the woods.

◆ ◆ ◆

Nell and her father led the villagers through the forest. They were weaving in-and-out of the trees, struggling to get through the dense forest as quickly as they could. Behind them, the Gnomes merely knocked trees over as they stomped through the woods.

The villagers stopped when they came to a tall pile of discarded trees. It seemed like an insurmountable mountain blocking their path.

Nell's father bent at the waist, gasping for air. Nell stopped beside him.

"Go," he said. "Go, sweetheart. I'll catch up."

Nell could hear the Gnomes approaching. She grabbed her dad by the hand and started pulling him toward the mountain of dead trees. She wasn't strong enough to move him, but he found new strength when he realized his daughter wasn't going anywhere without him.

They lost time as they climbed, but everyone eventually made it over the fallen trees and onto the wide path the Gnomes had cut through the forest. The terrain was much easier to cover now, but the adults had spent so much energy in their escape that they had little left. Many of them were falling behind. Some of them had stopped running entirely.

Nell yanked on her father's arm, desperate to pull him along.

"Daddy!" she screamed. *"Please! We have to go!"*

The Gnomes punched through the pile. Trees splintered in every direction.

"No!"

The adults urged their kids to go without them, but the children wouldn't listen. Instead, they put themselves between the adults and the attacking Gnomes.

The Gnomes slowed their approach. Their confidence was obvious. It wouldn't be much of a fight without the Tin Man and his hammer there to interfere.

Accepting his fate, Nell's father walked to his daughter's side and took her hand. “I'm sorry, baby girl. We'll find another way. I promise.”

Other parents moved forward to join their children. Eventually, they were all holding hands together, a small village standing together against evil.

“I love you, Nell.”

“I love you–”

Nell stopped short, watching as a tree limb lowered into view behind the approaching Gnomes. A pair of blinking eyes appeared in the tree's trunk, then its branches curled into a powerful hand that snatched one of the Gnomes from behind. Another tree grabbed the Gnome by his feet. In an instant, the towering trees had broken the stone creature in two.

The other Gnomes turned to watch, terrified as angry eyes began to appear in the trunks of all of the trees surrounding them.

“No! No! Don't!”

But the Gnomes pleas went unheard. The trees had vengeance in their hearts. One at a time they began snatching Gnomes off their feet. Some were tossed into the air; others were bashed against the ground; more still were broken to pieces as the trees unleashed their rage.

It was an ugly scene, but Nell couldn't take her eyes away. Eventually, when the Gnomes were nearly gone, she looked up at her dad and smiled, squeezing his hand as hard as she could, quietly vowing that she would never let go.

◆ ◆ ◆

Taylor stopped at a gnarled tree just off the path she and Wesley were taking through the woods. She looked back they way they'd come then shifted her attention into the tree's branches.

"What are you doing?" Wesley asked. "Why'd we stop?"

"C'mon! Up here!"

"No way!"

But Taylor was already on her way up the rugged tree trunk despite Wesley's protest. When she found a secure spot she turned to look down at him.

"You can do it, Wes. I've seen you. Trust me, it's easy."

"I know I can do it!" Wesley snapped. He stepped toward the tree and reached for the lowest branch before stopping. "Wait! We'll be trapped!"

"He can't climb–"

"But he'll wait for us to come down!"

Both kids looked up with a start when they heard tree limbs breaking behind them: the Gnome was coming.

Tay began to climb higher. "Do what you want, Wes."

Wesley eyed the tree with trepidation. He could hear the Gnome's labored breathing as it came up the path and looked up just in time to see him come into view. He had waited too long. Climbing the tree was no longer an option.

Wesley bolted down the path. He hoped it would branch off or circle back into the meadow so he'd have a better chance at escape. Instead, he began to slow when he saw the path dead-end just ahead of him. Only it didn't just stop. The path seemed to disappear. Wesley inched forward. The dirt path had led him to the steep cliff of a huge gorge. There was a small lagoon in the ravine below that was fed by a massive waterfall in the distance.

Panicked, Wesley turned to leave but saw the Gnome was already there to block his escape. Wes looked about. The forest was too dense to enter on either side of him.

The Gnome coiled his whip as he stepped forward.

"Dang it," Wesley muttered.

He looked over his shoulder. The drop was more than two hundred feet.

A loud pop echoed in Wesley's ear just before a hot spike of pain traveled the length of his spine and into his limbs. He reached around and felt warm blood trickling through the shirt on his back. Wes turned. The Gnome's gaping mouth had twisted into a toothless grin as he reeled his whip in, ready to lash it out again. This time, the Gnome struck the dirt at Wesley's feet. Wesley jumped away. He was convinced that just the crack of the Gnome's whip had made his back hurt more than it already did.

Wesley backed away, heels on the cliff's ledge. The Gnome lurched forward. He snapped the whip again. Wes tried to hold his ground but flinched.

His sneakers sent loose dirt and rock over the cliff's edge. Then–

"Look out below!"

Taylor swung down on a vine. Her legs flailed as she sailed toward the Gnome, but she straightened them just in time to kick him over the cliff. She dropped to the ground then hurried to Wesley's side. Both watched as the stone creature tumbled head-over-heels through the air before splashing into the water below.

"Dang," Taylor said. "That was close, huh?" She patted Wesley on the back. "I told you to climb the tree."

He looked at Taylor sharply. Her amused expression disappeared the moment she saw anger in his eyes.

"What? I'm kidding. You know that."

He pushed past her and started down the trail.

"Wesley? *What?*"

He never turned. All she saw was his back.

CHAPTER 14

THE LIBRARIAN COULD see much of Oz from his cell in the Witch's highest tower. While the sky was still overcast, a long pillar of morning light had pushed through grey clouds in the distance. It wasn't much, but the faint glimpse of sunlight felt like a good sign despite the fact he'd been captured and was badly wounded. It was the first he'd seen the sun since he arrived.

Someone came into the room, and the old man moved to the back of his cell. Earlier, they'd sent a young woman to tend to the wound in his shoulder. Later, two Munchkins brought him a plate with dry bread and a cup of vile liquid. But *this* visitor wasn't there to help. This time, it was Douglas Stanford who'd come to see him. He was reading something on his phone's screen as he casually walked into the room.

"I see you've corrupted Oz with cell phones," The Librarian said.

"You never were much for technology, were you?" Douglas held the phone up. "It's what they call a combo device. Almost like a walkie-talkie. I can call or text anyone who has a phone like this one within range."

The Librarian furrowed his brow.

"Have they been good to you? I asked them to bring you food and water."

"Why? You know I'm only here to stop you."

"That doesn't mean I want you *hurt*."

"No, of course not."

The old man gently massaged the wound beneath the heavy bandage on his arm: a reminder of the torture he'd suffered at Douglas's command.

Douglas let his eyes drift down to the wound, and his expression turned sad. "Sometimes I get carried away."

"I don't think so. You've grown into a very calculating man. You knew exactly what you were doing. You decided what you wanted a long time ago. Now you'll do anything to get it. If you have to break a few rules, you will. If you have to destroy the library you love, that's okay. And... if a day comes when you have to torture an old teacher, well... you'll do that, too."

"I'm treating the library about as well as it ever treated me."

The Librarian winced as he sat down on the small cot in his cell. "You know? Your son looks a lot like you did at his age. He's different, though. You were a lot more like that Bates boy."

"Leave my son out of this," Douglas said coolly.

"Is he here?"

"Randy's fine. So are the others, in case you're wondering."

The Librarian came off his cot and stepped toward the iron bars of his cell.

"What others?"

Douglas shook his head. "Why are you always surprised when kids have a hard time turning their back on all of this. Kids always want what they can't have. And this?" He gestured toward the window. "It's the biggest cookie jar of all time. Even *I* couldn't resist when I was their age."

Worry washed over The Librarian.

"I can't believe *you* came back," Douglas said. "Didn't you give your amulet to the Bates boy?"

"How could you possibly know that?"

Douglas didn't answer.

The old man looked down at his feet and sighed. “I assumed you were holding an amulet of your own. I was hoping we'd go back together.”

Douglas laughed and shook his head at the old man.

“Don't do this,” The Librarian pleaded. “You know how fragile the connection between the worlds can be. It doesn’t take much to–”

“The Elders have allowed me to come this far.”

“They’ve allowed you to come this far because you’ve threatened their lives and promised them riches. Did you forget they’re the only reason you’re here?”

Douglas let his gaze drift to the floor. “I know that. This isn’t your fault. I’ve never once blamed you. But don't get in my way more than you already have.”

“It doesn’t matter who you bring – the Headless Horseman, the Wicked Witch, it doesn't matter – you can build an army of villains if you like, but when you come into the catacombs, I'll be standing where I belong: between you and *The Book of Real*.”

Douglas shook his head. “I'm only taking what you promised me. I wouldn't–”

The old man cut him off. "You misunderstood, and apparently, the Elders have forgotten. The book isn't mine to give. I'm only there to protect it – it and everything inside the library. It's a job that should have been yours, if only..."

"If only *what?*"

"If only you'd earned it."

Douglas stared through the bars at his former teacher with his jaw clenched. His face reddened. He tried to hold onto his anger, but eventually it erupted and spewed viciously from within.

"No one deserves this more than me!"

He grabbed the cell bars and shook them so violently The Librarian thought he might rattle them loose, step into the cell, and beat him to death.

"You know what I've lost! I've given more than any of you!"

The old man backed away from the cell door.

"It's my turn! Do you hear me? It's my time, and I'm going to take back everything that was stolen from me. Everything!"

Douglas stormed out of the room, and The Librarian heaved a sigh of relief.

CHAPTER 15

THE VILLAGERS REGROUPED in the valley shortly after their victory over the Gnomes. Many rested in the shade of a tarp from the wagon; others ate crusts of bread the children had stuffed in their pockets before leaving the village; children played on the grinding machine, beating it with sticks as if slaying an evil dragon.

Taylor walked through the makeshift camp to an area near the tree line where the Cowardly Lion was lying in the grass and licking his wounds. The Munchkin maiden was nearby too, inspecting the damage done to the Tin Man's body by the Gnomes.

"Is he okay?" Taylor asked.

"Not to worry," the Tin Man explained. "I only have a few dents in my torso. Nothing that can't be fixed with a little hammer work."

"Don't worry! I'm going to take good care of him," the maiden exclaimed. She took the Tin Man's hand. There was a sparkle in her eye that dimmed as she realized her fiancé did not share her joy.

"Come," he said. "There's something we must discuss."

The Scarecrow joined their small group just as the Tin Man led the maiden away. "Where are they going?"

"I'm not sure," Taylor said.

"I've never seen a man made of metal before. Is there a race of metal men living in Oz that I don't know about?"

"No," Taylor said. "He's one of a kind."

"Oh," the Scarecrow said. "That's not too unusual. I think I am, too. One of a kind, that is. Unless you've seen another talking scarecrow walking around."

Taylor watched the Tin Man and maiden until they disappeared into the forest. Once they were gone, she turned to face the Scarecrow.

"I haven't," she said. "I think you're the only one."

While the Lion looked quite normal - much like the lions she'd seen in the Astoria zoo - the Scarecrow definitely belonged in the fairy tale land. He looked like a stuffed toy come to life. He wore a farmer's plaid shirt and denim overalls. Straw poked out from beneath his collar and at the end of his sleeves. He had button eyes that never blinked, and the rest of his features were sewn onto his cloth face with colorful yarn.

Wesley walked over and joined them.

"Hey," Taylor said. "I was just going to–"

"Aren't you going to introduce me?" Wesley snapped.

Taylor recoiled a bit. Wesley's cold demeanor had morphed into something different since their battle with the Gnomes. He seemed angry now - as if he was looking for a fight.

"I was getting there." She gestured toward Wesley beside her. "Guys? This is my best friend, Wesley. We're... well... we know Dorothy."

"We don't *know* her," Wesley corrected.

Taylor looked over at Wesley and arched her eyebrows. He knew she wasn't one to stretch the truth. This was already difficult. Why was he trying to make things more difficult? Was he looking to start a fight with *her*?

"Well," she stammered. "We don't *know* her. But... we're from the same place."

"Kansas?"

"Near there," Taylor said.

The Scarecrow let his head hang. "I'm sorry, but I'm afraid I'm the bearer of terrible news. Dorothy was... she was killed in a valley not far from here."

"P-please don't t-talk about this," the Lion said. "I'm not sure I c-can take it again."

Taylor patted the Lion's side. "That's okay. We already know what happened."

"How?" the Scarecrow asked.

Taylor looked over at Wesley for approval. He made an exaggerated gesture toward the Scarecrow and shook his head. She'd known him long enough to read his body language with ease...

You've already lied once, Tay. Might as well do it again.

"Well," Taylor began, "you can't tell anyone... but... the Wizard in Emerald City sent us to help you. It's a long story. We have a lot to talk about."

◆ ◆ ◆

The Tin Man and the Munchkin maiden found privacy away from the others in the forest. They sat together on the trunk of an old, hollowed-out tree.

The maiden held the Tin Man's hand in her lap as they talked.

"I knew you'd come," she explained. "I told the others. They didn't believe me, but I wouldn't let myself despair the way I did before." The Tin Man looked sad. "What is it? What's wrong, my love?"

He sighed. "We're going to go through something very hard. But you're not alone. Okay? Not this time. These people are–"

"I have you. I–"

"I can't stay."

His words put fear in her eyes. Suddenly panicked, she began to fidget, blinking wildly and playing with her hair as she fought a rush of fresh tears. "W-what are you talking about? Of course you can stay."

"Do you remember the children who brought us together? Taylor and Wesley? The kids who found me in the forest?"

"How could I forget?"

"They've told me they can fix things in Oz – make everything go back to the way it was before."

"But... that's wonderful!"

"I have to go with them."

The color drained from the maiden's face. “No!” she whimpered. “No! No! No! I won't allow it.” She pulled his hand into her chest. “You can't leave me. We've already been through too much–”

“Don’t you see? That's why I have to go. Others in Oz are suffering just as we did. What if I can help them?”

“Let someone else. You've done enough. You're a hero to these people now. Let someone else save Oz.”

“I'm not a hero,” he said. “I've done things, love. Terrible things. Things a man with a heart could never do.”

“We've told you. Your heart has nothing to do with who you are.”

“But I believe it does.”

The maiden saw the Tin Man would not give in and came to her feet. “Fine,” she said. “Then I'll go with you. We can save Oz together.”

“You can't,” he whispered.

“Why not?” she shrieked. She was yelling loud enough now that the others in camp could probably hear.

"I only know what I was told. No one can come. Only Taylor, the Scarecrow, the Cowardly Lion, and myself. That's how it's supposed to be."

"And what is it you're supposed to do?"

The Tin Man looked down at his feet. "We're going to kill the Wicked Witch of the West."

"Oh no! No! Run away with me. We'll go some-place far away, leave everything behind just like we planned." Her words were running together in desperation. She caressed his cheek. He took her hands away.

"I can't, my love. Don't you understand? If I leave Oz like this, if I do nothing to help defeat the evil in our land, I won't be any different than those who walked past my frozen body in the forest."

Without thinking, he moved a hand to wipe the tears from her face but pulled away. Even her tears would be enough to rust his joints.

"I will come back for you. I promise."

"I've heard that before," she said angrily.

The Tin Man flinched. "Please understand."

He kissed her hand gently then started to walk away. He was halfway down the path when she yelled out after him. "I won't!" she cried.

The Tin Man looked back over his shoulder. "What?"

"I won't forgive you."

"You don't mean that. We're–"

"Soulmates?" She shook her head. "Only someone without a heart could do this to the woman he loves! *People* have soulmates. You're something else. Good luck to you... *Tin Man.*"

His shoulders slumped into a frown as he trudged away. When he was gone, the Munchkin maiden began to sob.

◆ ◆ ◆

Taylor and Wes were still talking with the others when the Tin Man reappeared from the woods. Most in camp had heard the tail end of their argument and tried to avert their eyes, but Wesley walked over to greet his sad-looking friend.

"What happened? You okay?"

The Tin Man gestured toward the Scarecrow and Lion. "Have they agreed to help?"

Wesley nodded. "It looks that way."

"Good," the Tin Man said. "I will as well, but you must take me from this place. If I stay, I can't promise I won't change my mind."

Wesley hurried back to Taylor.

"What happened?" she asked.

"He says he'll go. We just have to get out of here. Like... now." He turned to the Scarecrow. "Can you take us to the spot where Dorothy was killed?"

The Scarecrow scratched his head. "I don't know that I can remember exactly where Dorothy fell. My memory isn't very good."

The Lion sighed. "We can s-show you where she's b-b-buried."

That was close enough for Tay. She looked over at Wesley.

"Will you tell Hope it's time to go?"

Wesley smirked, saluting Taylor sarcastically before he left.

She shook her head. She didn't know what had gotten into Wesley, but she knew this wasn't the right time to address it.

Taylor saw the Munchkin maiden come out of the forest. She was crying and shaking so badly that a few of the village women went over to help her back into camp. Taylor looked over at the Tin Man.

He was collecting his things and seemed intent on keeping his back turned to the maiden. Her heart ached for them. She knew this was the right thing to do – but why the heck did it have to hurt so bad?

CHAPTER 16

THE LIBRARIAN PUSHED his hand through the bars on his cell. He was surprised to see just how easily he could access the lock. Now, if only he had something to jimmy it open.

He scanned the floor. He'd read enough bad novels to know breaking out would be easy if the girl who'd wrapped his shoulder had left a needle behind or if the Munchkins had accidentally dropped a fork. But there was nothing.

The Librarian fell to one knee, hoping to find his bed's frame was held together with nails or screws – anything he could pry loose and use to pick the lock. Instead, he found the cot's frame was carved from a single piece of wood. There were no seams to speak of – no metal pieces holding it together at all.

He stood up, kicking at the bed in frustration.

Think, old man. Think!

He took off his wire spectacles and was wiping them with the tail of his shirt when something occurred to him. He reached through the bars to feel the lock once more, this time taking an extra moment to measure the keyhole's shape and size with his fingertips. When finished, he began to bend the wire frames on his glasses out of shape. He made the earpiece as long and as pointed as possible then shoved his glasses through the cell bars. When his fingers found the lock again he carefully jammed the earpiece from his glasses into the keyhole and began to jimmy the lock as best he could.

◆ ◆ ◆

Dorothy's was a shallow grave: nothing but loose dirt and rock. The Scarecrow had taken some straw from beneath his shirt to mark the grave with the farm girl's name, but the wind had blown most of that away in the days since.

Taylor stood beside Wes. Dorothy's companions were on the opposite side of the grave. As they paid their respects, a terrible reality was setting in for

Tay. There was a real danger here. Any one of them could end up in a grave just like this one.

"Can you tell us what happened?" Wesley asked.

"It was d-dreadful," the Lion said. "The worst thing I ever s-saw! Ever!"

The Scarecrow picked up where the Lion left off. "We left Emerald City for the Witch's castle. You see? I have no brains."

"And I, n-n-no courage."

"But the Wizard, he told us if we killed the Witch he would give us the brains and the courage we lack. So that's what we set off to do."

"He can give you such things?" the Tin Man asked.

"I assume so. Why would he promise us something he couldn't give?"

"Do you think he might help give me the heart I need to love my fiancée again?"

"You never know," Wesley said.

"Maybe this *is* my destiny."

The Scarecrow continued. "I don't know *how*, but the Witch saw us coming. She sent wolves and crows, anything she thought might stop us. And then... she sent the bees."

"Th-they s-stung her to d-d-death!" The Lion leaned forward and hid his face behind large paws. "I know I'm a c-coward. Everyone says I'm afraid of my shadow, but it was the w-worst thing I ever s-saw. I don't want to go back. I can't!"

"We have to," the Scarecrow said. "For Dorothy." He lowered his gaze to the young girl's grave. "She was the bravest little girl. I wish I were smart enough to explain it. She was just so special."

"You did fine," the Tin Man explained.

Taylor watched the characters converse as if they were lifelong friends. "Can you think of a way you might have helped if you'd been there? A way we can beat the Bees if they come again?" Tay was leading the Tin Man with her question, but she needed to get him working on a solution now. The Tin Man was their only hope against the Bees, and they would only get one shot at this.

"I only know that the Bees won't be able to sting me as I am made of tin." He stopped to think. "And won't they die if their stingers break off?"

"I don't rightly know," the Scarecrow said.

"I think I've heard that before."

"P-perhaps we can convince the b-bees to sting you first. B-b-but how would we d-do that? It's impossible!" Talk of the Black Bees sent a wave of panic surging through the Lion all over again.

"We have time to come up with something," Taylor said.

"Tay's right," Wesley added. "I'm sure we'll figure it out on the way."

"*You* aren't going. We decided. Remember?"

Taylor started to walk away. Wesley looked over at Hope. She encouraged him to keep going with a nod in Taylor's direction.

"No, we didn't."

Taylor turned. "What?"

"*You* decided. It's not the same thing. You never asked me if I was okay with it."

"You didn't *say* anything."

"Would it have mattered?" he asked sharply.

"Well... I..."

"I mean, I said I didn't want to free the Tin Man. Remember that? It didn't matter *then*, why would it matter *now*?"

"This isn't some backyard adventure, Wes. You might have died if–"

"If you didn't save me?"

She prickled at his tone. There was loathing in his voice. He'd never talked to her like this before.

"What's *wrong* with you?"

Wesley blew out a quick laugh. "What? Did you think I was only going to stand up to *some* of the bullies in my life? At least when Randy bullies me he's up front about it."

"What are you talking about? I'm always the first one to stand up for you when Randy's around!"

"Yeah? And *why's that*?"

"What?"

"You don't do it for *me*. You do it so you'll have another story to tell." He looked around at the others and shifted his tone to mock Taylor. "Hey! Look everyone! I just saved Wesley Bates from a beating! Isn't he lucky to have me?"

The others seemed embarrassed. They shifted their feet and looked at the ground with no idea how to respond.

"Wes, I never–"

"You don't *have* to say it, Taylor. You act like you're better than *everyone*. You're always telling me what's right, what's wrong, what I should have done. Well, you know what? This time *you* should have listened to *me*!"

There'd been a special chemistry between them once; something new and exciting that felt electric.

Now, it was different. Every word out of his mouth was a shock to her system, lashing out, probing, looking for the perfect place to strike.

"I'm sorry. It's just," Taylor gestured toward Dorothy Gale's grave, "she *died*, Wes."

"Yeah?" he sneered. "And whose fault is that?"

His words crackled, finally striking where Taylor would feel it most.

Strangely though, this was exactly what she needed. She'd known all along that Wesley should stay behind, but selfishly, she'd allowed him to tag along. He made her feel strong, like she could take on anything Oz threw at her. But not anymore. Now all she wanted to do was run away and leave him. He would hate her, but at least he'd be safe. She'd been feeling the tug-o-war conflict between right and wrong since they'd left school, but it was finally over. The rope had snapped. No one had won. There was no right or wrong decision, only what Taylor knew she had to do. Wesley was right...

Sometimes you've got to break the rules to do the right thing.

"You're right," she whispered. "I should have listened. None of this would have happened if we'd done what you said. I just... I don't want anyone else to get hurt because of me. You know?"

Wes frowned. "You couldn't have known all this would happen, Tay."

His tone was softening. She could see Wesley already regretted the things he'd said and how he'd said them. He wouldn't apologize, but the look on his face said enough. It's what she would hold onto after she was gone.

"Besides," Wesley began, "if we're gonna fix this we gotta do it together, right? Like always."

Taylor forced a smile. "You're right," she said. "You and me. Together like always."

◆ ◆ ◆

Taylor was awake, laying on a woven blanket and staring up at the night sky. She found if she kept her eyes on the heavens she could almost forget she was still trapped in a nightmare of her own creation.

The Tin Man was propped up against a tree, sitting upright while he slept. The Cowardly Lion was curled up near the dying fire, snoring so loudly Taylor wondered how anyone could sleep at all.

Taylor sat up and saw Wesley had fallen asleep beneath a large oak. It had been several hours since their fight, but his words had cut deeply enough that the wounds were still fresh. Her emotions had been on a roller coaster ride ever since. There were times she wanted to hug him and apologize, but there were moments when she felt like punching him in the face. Through it all, she felt sick to her stomach, just as she had after her father's outburst in the kitchen.

Only this was worse.

A few weeks after his move to Astoria, Wesley had made Tay watch an old, black-and-white movie called *Invasion of the Body Snatchers*. He said it was a classic. In it, aliens kidnapped humans then replaced them with look-a-likes that acted nothing like the originals. That's how her father had been: snatched. He looked the same, but everything inside – all the important stuff – was different.

But Wesley's body hadn't been snatched. He hadn't changed on Tay like everyone else. He'd been with Taylor when the library shifted. This was the real Wesley Bates; and the real Wesley Bates thought Taylor was a self-centered bully. She had never cared what anyone thought. She'd heard all the names whispered behind her back – teacher's pet, goodie-goodie, snob – but only this one hurt, and it hurt because it had come from him. It had come from Wes.

She rose to her feet, and dusted off her shorts before quietly walking over to the spot where Wesley slept. She stood in silence, watching her friend sleep. Were they still friends? Strangely, it was only now when he seemed to hate her that she realized she wanted something more from him than friendship. A lot more.

“Why are you up?”

Taylor turned to find Hope standing just a few feet behind her. The moonlight shone through the trees and cast a web of dark shadows across her face.

“Don't wake him,” Taylor pleaded.

“You're leaving, aren't you?”

Taylor looked down at Wes. “Tell him I'm not mad. He'll think that's why I left, but that isn’t true. I just don’t want him to get hurt.”

Wesley rolled onto his back so Taylor could see his face. He looked lost in a bad dream. Taylor knelt beside him. She saw his glasses were folded neatly on top of the backpack beside him.

“He looks so mature without his glasses,” Taylor whispered. She pushed the hair from Wesley's face but made sure not to wake him. “I like him better with them on. Don't you?” Hope didn't answer. “I wish I would have told him that.”

Taylor came to her feet. “Take him home. Wait in the library like you said. I never should have let you guys come this far.”

“Are you sure this is what you want to do?”

Taylor looked back at Wesley. “He just got his life together.”

Hope watched Taylor walk over to the Cowardly Lion where she began to stroke his golden mane. A moment later, he woke and nearly jumped out of his skin.

“Shh!” Taylor said. “Were you having a bad dream?”

“That's all I ever have,” the beast whimpered. “Is it time to go?”

Taylor nodded. The Lion stood up on all fours, arching his back and baring his teeth in an exaggerated yawn.

“Can you wake the Tin Man?” Taylor asked.

The Lion gave a slight nod then padded away.

"Remember to be quiet," Taylor explained. "We don't want to wake anyone else."

❖ ❖ ❖

Rough pressure on Wesley's neck pulled him from sleep. He woke to find Hope glaring down at him.

"What's wrong?" he asked groggily, stretching as he wiped the sleep from his eyes. "Is everything okay?"

Hope stormed away without answering.

Wesley scrambled to his feet. He looked about in confusion. "Where's Tay?"

A flash of morning light glinted off something in Hope's hand and captured Wesley's full attention. The Librarian's amulet was dangling from her closed fist. Wesley moved a hand to his chest, making sure it was *his* amulet she was carrying. It was. The metal bookmark that had been hanging from his neck since they left the library was now gone.

"Hey!" Wesley said. "What are you doing?"

"I tried to do this the easy way," Hope explained. "The two of you just wouldn't listen."

"Where's Taylor?"

Hope threw a bag over her shoulder. "C'mon," she said. "Get your things together. We're going back."

"Did you hear me? *Where's Tay?*"

Hope sighed. "She went on without us. Just like she said she would."

"No... she... she said she *wasn't* going to do that."

"Grow up, Wes. Even the Scarecrow knew she was lying."

Wesley sprinted up the small hill that lay ahead of them. He hoped he would see Taylor on the other side. He didn't.

"Can you blame her for leaving?" Hope asked. "I can't believe the things you said to her. That's how you treat your friends?"

Wesley glared at Hope. She'd put those thoughts in his head.

"Hey, there's nothing I said you weren't already thinking. All I wanted was for you to show a little backbone so that she didn't get us all killed."

Wes began to replay his argument with Taylor in his head. Why had he said those things? He hadn't meant any of them. It felt like a punch to the gut knowing those were the last things he'd said to Taylor.

"We're going after her," Wesley said. "Get your stuff." He hurried to put on his backpack. Hope didn't move. *"Did you hear me?"*

"If only you could have stood up to *her* like this."

"Fine," Wesley said. "Give me that. I'll go myself."

He marched toward Hope and tried to snatch the amulet from her grip, but she held it above her head and out of reach.

"How's she supposed to get back?"

Hope thought before answering. "*Mr. Stanford* will bring her home."

"Mr. Stanford? Why would Randy's dad..."

He didn't finish. Wesley had spent so much time focused on the Oz puzzle, he'd neglected their own story. Regardless, the pieces had fallen into place without him: Hope's erratic behavior, her use of a cell phone in Oz, her constant criticism of Taylor and how she'd used those ideas to drive a wedge between the two friends, her obsession with The Librarian's amulet. Alone they had revealed little, but now, together, those pieces were painting a focused picture that was hard to deny.

"You're working with Mr. Stanford?"

"I'd love to say I was here to protect you, but this is all I was after." She held the amulet up, and Wes felt like he'd taken another body blow.

"If it helps, Douglas *really will* bring her back. I promise. He's a good man. He's waiting for her now. We'll meet them tonight, and you can tell her just how sorry you are. We're girls, Wes. We get over this stuff pretty fast."

"What about The Librarian?"

She shook her head. "He won't be so lucky."

Wesley couldn't believe it. How could he be so stupid? It was right there in front of him the whole time. Of course Douglas had someone working on the inside. It's exactly how Wes would have written it.

He shifted his gaze to the horizon.

"Don't even think about it," Hope said sternly.

"I'm supposed to trust you?"

"It's your only option."

He didn't respond.

"They've got a head start. You won't catch them."

He didn't answer.

"She doesn't want you around!"

He winced.

"You've seen what this place has become, Wesley. People are dying." She softened her voice. "You won't make it."

Wes turned and leveled cold eyes to meet hers.

"What happens if you don't find her? What happens if you get lost?" She showed him the amulet once more. "You can't open the portal home without me. You get left behind, and she'll blame herself for that, too. Is that really how you want all this to end?"

Wesley looked to the ground for answers that weren't there. Hope offered her hand. He could almost feel its pull on him. He reached for it, sure it would bring relief the minute he was in her grip. But then, something occurred to him and he abruptly pulled away. Something Taylor had said about him in the library...

Wesley's a writer, the memory echoed. *A great one.*

He backed away.

"Wesley? Don't–"

"She doesn't get to leave me," Wesley said. "She doesn't get to leave me, and this story isn't over until I tell her that."

With that, he turned his back on Hope and began to run away, slowly at first, but quickening his pace with every stride. Hope watched him crest the hill, her hand out until he disappeared on the other side.

She never saw Wesley Bates again.

CHAPTER 17

DOUGLAS CAME ONTO the castle's balcony and found the Witch waiting for him with her back to the doorway. "You sent for me?"

"I did," the Witch replied.

"I take it you've made a decision, then."

The Witch didn't answer. Douglas saw she had her attention fixed on something in the distance. He joined her near the balcony's rail.

"I can see them, you know? They're coming again, just as you said they would."

Douglas followed her gaze. Thick patches of mist were still hanging in the air which allowed little visibility. He couldn't see anything beyond the canyon that guarded the Witch's castle.

"That wretched Woodsman is with them this time. And the girl, she's... *different*."

While she looked to be staring off into space, Douglas remembered *Oz* author L. Frank Baum had gifted her with an eye as powerful as a telescope. It enabled her to see anything happening within her kingdom.

The Witch threw her hands into the air and cackled laughter. "We'll just see about them. My Black Bees finished them once before. We can play this game over and over if they like." She snapped her fingers at a guard standing near the doorway. "Fetch my silver whistle! We'll just see about this!"

The guard scurried out of the room.

"The Bees won't be enough," Douglas explained.

"Really?" the Witch croaked. "Tell me, dear. Is that in your little book, too? They worked just fine the last time."

"They did," Douglas answered. "But can a bee sting a man made of metal?" The Witch's sneer weakened as she looked out into the murk again. "I won't wait forever. I'm sure *someone* in Oz would love a chance to obtain the power I'm offering."

The Witch scowled at his subtle threat, but her attention shifted when the guard returned. She took the whistle and blew it, and a high-pitched whine sounded through Winkie Country.

Moments later, the Bees appeared in a massive swarm on the horizon. The swarm looked like a black cloud moving toward them at impossible speeds. It rustled and buzzed and seemed to dance on the air. When the lead Bees turned, the rest followed in a surge that sent a wave of color and shape cascading from one side of the cloud to the next. It was like a waltz or a tango, one of nature's most dazzling displays. It was a dance deserving of beautiful music, but there was nothing but the dreadful drone.

When they arrived, the swarm's sound was so intense Douglas was sure his ears would rupture. He covered them just as a giant bee appeared from within the swarm: the Queen.

“Go to the strangers!” the Witch howled over their buzz. She pointed the way. “Kill them all this time, and don't come back 'til you have!”

The Queen turned to lead her swarm. While most were the size of a balled fist, the Queen was only a little smaller than a tricycle Douglas had bought Randy on his first birthday. She had red eyes, yellow stripes, and a stinger that looked like it could easily rip a person in two.

Douglas watched them leave, and for a moment, he was sure the swarm took the shape of an arrow aimed in the direction the Witch had pointed – toward Taylor Morales and her fairy-tale friends.

◆ ◆ ◆

The Witch's castle appeared to Wesley shortly after he left camp. It seemed to float on the horizon, the sky behind it the color of a fresh bruise. Seeing it gave Wesley some relief, but only a little. He knew he was heading in the right direction; but that didn't mean he was on the right path. If Taylor and the others were heading toward the castle from a different angle, he would never catch them, no matter how much faster he was moving than his friends.

Regardless, Wes continued in quick fits and starts through the wasteland. He only slowed to a quick walk when he needed rest. Then, after a brief respite, he'd push himself to run again. He'd been on the go for about an hour when the sight of bloodstained grass brought him to a sudden halt.

Fear raised a lump in his throat. He inched forward, eyes squeezed shut, needing to see but refusing to look. He finally forced his eyes open when his sneakers hit something wet.

Wesley was standing in a puddle of blood with the headless carcass of a dead wolf at his feet. He looked about. Dozens of dead wolves lay at his feet, each with a ragged wound where its head should have been. He looked down and saw one of the wolf heads near his foot. Horrified, he kicked it away with a grimace.

This was a scene that had been too dark to include in the movie, but Wesley knew it well. In the book, the Wicked Witch sent all manner of creatures to stop Dorothy and her companions from reaching the castle. The first beasts dispatched were the forty wolves at Wesley's feet.

But something wasn't sitting well with Wes. In the book, the Tin Man killed the wolves with his axe. So how had Dorothy and the others made it past the pack without him? How had they even made it to the bees in the first place?

Wesley stepped through the clearing, doing his best to avoid the carnage along the ground. He and Taylor had come to fix the *Oz* tale, and while they had done much to correct the story's course, that didn't mean events ahead would unfold exactly as expected. Somehow, Dorothy and her companions had found a way to defeat the wolves without the Tin Man's help. In this new version of *Oz*, there was no reason to think the bees couldn't turn the tables on Taylor. Maybe having the Tin Man wouldn't be enough. Maybe Taylor was heading for trouble they couldn't even imagine.

Wesley looked up at the castle then lowered his head and began to run again. He was incredibly tired, but he was prepared to push himself a bit harder the rest of the way.

◆ ◆ ◆

Randy and Bones joined Douglas. Together, they followed the Witch into a dome-shaped room with a massive crystal ball as its focal point. The huge ball was perfectly clear and rested on an ornate stand that was carved from dark wood remarkably similar to the wood used for the woodcarvings in Astoria's library.

The Witch began to stroke the impressive piece. As soon as her wrinkled hand was atop the ball, a cloud of pink smoke appeared within the crystal and began to swirl like a storm taking shape.

Douglas and Randy stepped forward to join the Witch just as the pink smoke settled near the bottom of the sphere to reveal four figures standing within the haze: the Tin Man, the Scarecrow, the Cowardly Lion, and–

"Dad!" Randy exclaimed. "That's Taylor!"

Douglas raised a hand to his son. The boy fell silent.

"Here they come," the Witch said in her sinister voice. A piece of pink smoke broke free from the cloud. Randy watched the smoke turn black before taking shape as the Witch's swarm of killer bees.

She snarled into the crystal orb. "You strangers will wish you *never* returned!"

◆ ◆ ◆

Taylor looked back, checking the way they'd come. The sun was rising quickly now. She knew Wesley was probably awake and wondered how he'd taken the news of her midnight departure.

"It won't be as hard if you stop looking back," the Tin Man said. "Not looking back has helped me. Well, it's helped *some*."

Taylor offered an understanding nod. She patted the Tin Man on his back and was about to say something when the Cowardly Lion cut her off with a meek roar.

"Look," the Scarecrow cried. His arm flopped as he pointed at something in the sky ahead. "They're coming! Just like before! Just like you said! They're here!"

All four looked toward the swarm of Black Bees approaching in the distance. It was moving straight for them, pulsing, ready to consume anything in its path.

"W-what are we g-going to d-do?!"

"What do *you* think we should do?" Taylor asked the Scarecrow.

"I'm the *last person* to ask!"

"No you're not," she said. "You can do it. Think! How can we force them to sting the Tin Man?" Though she couldn't explain why, Taylor felt it was important the companions find a solution for the bees on their own.

The Scarecrow shuffled from foot to foot. "Umm... umm..."

The bees were closing. The Lion hurried over and poked his round face into their conversation. "They're c-coming!" he said. "We n-n-need to hide!"

"That's it!" the Scarecrow exclaimed.

"W-w-what?!"

"Hide!"

The Scarecrow unfastened two buttons on his shirt and quickly began to yank straw from beneath it. "The two of you can hide beneath my straw," he explained. "The bees won't see you, and I'll be nothing but a pile of old clothes." He pointed to the Tin Man. "They'll go straight for him!"

Taylor checked the swarm.

They had two minutes.

Maybe three.

"C-can't the b-bees smell fear?" the Lion quaked.

"No!" Taylor rushed over to the Scarecrow. "C'mon! I'll help!"

◆ ◆ ◆

"What are they doing?" the Witch asked. Her eyes were still fixed on the miniature beings inside her crystal ball, but she sounded nervous. "My bees will want to finish the Scarecrow, too."

"They're going to hide beneath his straw," Douglas said.

"But why? My bees will seek them out."

"But they'll sting the Tin Man first. And what happens to a bee when his stinger breaks?"

Worry washed over the Witch, and Douglas knew she finally understood the Tin Man's importance and how he would affect events to come.

❖ ❖ ❖

Taylor could hear the swarm's deafening buzz – even from beneath the haystack she and the Lion were hiding under.

"Can you see us?" Taylor asked.

The Tin Man stepped back to examine his work. "I can see his tail."

"T-t-tuck it in!"

The Tin Man did as he was told then turned to face the onslaught. The swarm raced toward him then came to an abrupt halt, stopping to hover just short of the metal man.

"They've seen us," the Lion said. He was chewing nervously on the tip of his tail.

"No they haven't," Taylor whispered. "Shh!"

The Tin Man watched as the Queen appeared from within the swarm. The giant bee hovered before him, measuring the Tin Man as if curious to know why he wasn't running away. She moved forward, circling to see how he would react. When the Tin Man didn't move, the Queen darted toward him. Her rear twisted so that her stinger took the lead. She was vicious in her attack, striking her mark with fury.

But the Tin Man's chest didn't give way as expected. The Queen bellowed in pain, her mammoth stinger bent in half as she sputtered toward the ground.

The swarm swelled in size as it filled with rage. It rushed toward the Tin Man and instantly consumed him in a teeming, black mass.

Taylor carefully pushed her face through the straw for a better view. The Tin Man had completely vanished in the swarm's attack. The throbbing cloud had enveloped his entire body. She saw glimpses of him, of course: a hand here, a bit of his leg there. Then, as the bees fought to avenge their Queen, the swarm began to shrink as bees fell to the wayside with broken stingers.

Taylor watched as the swarm slowly changed into a pile of dead bees at the Tin Man's feet. Her friend reappeared from within the madness. His chest was out, his chin held high. It was an image Taylor would cherish for the rest of her life. Books were better than movies, but both were fading stars next to the supernova known as real life.

She wished Wesley were there to see it.

CHAPTER 18

THE WITCH'S THIN lips quivered in anger as she watched the Tin Man help the other companions to their feet.

"Fools!" she screamed. "This isn't over! You hear me? I'll never stop. You should have learned your lesson the first time!"

Douglas stepped toward her. "Have you learned *your* lesson?"

The Witch turned to face him. When she saw him standing there, her anger began to fade. "It was exactly as you said," she muttered. "I will do as you ask. I am your servant." She lowered her head in a slight bow. "What would you have me do?"

Douglas waited to make sure the Witch was sincere before answering. She seemed to be. She never lifted her eyes. She stayed there, her head bowed as she waited for instructions.

"I know your instincts tell you to send your Winkie army, but something tells me they're a cowardly bunch and will only waste our time."

"I'm lucky they can push a broom," she agreed.

Douglas continued. "You have a Golden Cap that gives you control over the race of winged monkeys. Bring it to me."

The Witch looked up at him. "How do you... ah, yes... *your book*."

She snapped her fingers at a guard near the door. "The cap!" She used a demanding voice. It was probably an effort to remind those in the room that she still ruled, even if it seemed to some that Douglas might have taken her throne.

◆ ◆ ◆

Taylor finished stuffing straw beneath the Scarecrow's shirt, and he popped up to a sitting position. "Did it work?" he asked joyfully.

"It did," she answered.

"Yes," the Tin Man said. "That was a splendid idea."

"We didn't even d-die," the Lion added.

Everyone laughed. The Scarecrow's lips were sewn in the shape of a constant smile, but Taylor could tell news of his plan's success had made him happy.

The Scarecrow bounced to his feet. He pointed at the shadow of the Witch's castle looming on the horizon. "C'mon! I bet she's scared to death now! We don't want her to get away!"

Taylor watched as the Scarecrow led the Tin Man and the Cowardly Lion away. They were skipping through the meadow, all three ready to take on the world as a song from the 1939 movie began running through Tay's head.

They're going to be so disappointed, she thought.

The companions were ready to storm the Witch's castle, and while she suspected they might eventually make it, Taylor had a different destination in mind, a goal of her own.

And they were almost there.

◆ ◆ ◆

Randy followed Douglas and the Witch onto the castle's balcony. The Witch had replaced the pointed hat on her head with the Golden Cap. Made of an animal's hide, the cap was tall and rimmed at the bottom with a ruby-encrusted gold band. It looked heavy, but the Witch seemed to wear it with ease. As soon as it was in place, she began to chant spells in a language no one from Randy's world had ever spoken. *"Shekhanah! Retrasrak! Meilon!"* The Witch doubled over as if the spell caused her great pain. *"Ziz! Zuz! Meilon!"*

The sky turned green. The gold band along the bottom of the Witch's cap began to glow. And then, the winged monkeys came. Dozens of them.

Randy stepped closer to his dad. He'd done his best to appear brave through their journey, but he couldn't hide his fear any longer. The monkeys looked like one of the gruesome monsters drawn in a horror comic he'd stolen from Wesley's locker. Their faces were pink but seemed strangely human. They had floppy ears and rotten teeth. Each had long arms wrapped in dirty gauze with three-talon claws in place of hands. Randy could deal with most of this. Oddly, it was their wings that sickened his stomach. The giant wings spanned nearly ten feet and were covered in furry skin stretched so tautly it appeared translucent. Even worse, some of the wings had strange holes that looked like they were rimmed with black mold – as if they were infected with some strange virus that was eating away at their flesh a little at a time. Randy tried to look away, but the hideous wings kept drawing his gaze. He just couldn't help it.

One at a time the monkeys landed on the balcony's ledge. Then, a monkey wearing a small cap stepped forward, his sunken eyes fixed angrily on Douglas.

"Greetings," Douglas began. "We've called you here because–"

"Who are you?" the monkey demanded. "The winged monkeys answer *only* to Her Highness!"

Douglas drew a deep breath. "Actually, you answer to the owner of this cap." He held out his hand. Though reluctant, the Witch took the cap from her head and handed it over. Douglas tucked it beneath his arm.

The monkey's face twisted in frustration. "Very well."

"There are strangers approaching the castle," Douglas explained. "They are coming to *kill* Her Highness. I want you to go to them and bring the girl to me. Unharmed."

"What?" the Witch howled. *"I want that girl strung up! I want the flesh peeled from her—"*

Douglas silenced her with a cold look. "That little girl is from *my world*. She's not to be touched unless *I* say."

The Witch bowed her head. Douglas continued.

"The others will try to stop you," he told the monkey. "Do what you want with them but the girl is not to be hurt. Are we clear?"

"Indeed," the monkey said. "But understand this, it matters little who is wearing the cap. You have called us for the third and final time. Agreed?"

Douglas nodded without a word.

"Then we shall carry out your command to the letter." The monkey bowed his head just as the Witch had a moment before. This time, Douglas matched it with a slight nod of his own.

The monkeys took to the air and came together as a group in the distance. Their leader spoke briefly with his brethren, and they started away from the castle.

"Shall we return to my observation room?" the Witch asked. "We can watch just as we did with the bees."

"Why?" Douglas smirked. "I already know what happens."

CHAPTER 19

WESLEY HAD BEEN running off-and-on for most of the morning. The sun was high now and unbearably hot. His skin was covered in a slick sheen of sweat. His legs burned. A stitch in his side begged him to stop. Not that he would. He'd found the pile of bees, and it had filled him with new life. Not only did he know he was heading in the right direction, he knew he was close. A few of the bees had still been alive, bouncing around within the heap, their wings buzzing too weakly to take them off the ground as they went through their final death throes. Whatever happened had happened recently. Taylor couldn't be far.

He pushed on, only stopping when he came to a gravel path that disappeared into a deep ravine that cut through the countryside toward the Witch's castle.

The embankment leading into the ravine was steep. While there was a sparkling blue stream winding through the valley, much of the ravine was covered in dense undergrowth. Jagged rock shelves jutted out from the ground. Gnarled trees grew sideways from the ravine walls.

Wesley looked into the valley and used a hand to shield his eyes from the sun. Going into the ravine would be a huge waste of time if Taylor and the others hadn't done the same. But then–

His eyes lit up!

Taylor and the others were in the valley below.

He yelled into the wind: "Tay!" She didn't turn. "Taylor! Up here!"

He was so far away that the companions looked like four ants walking in single file along the ravine floor. It didn't matter, though. They were walking. He was running. He'd be with them in a matter of minutes. With Tay.

Wesley started down the path, minding his excitement, careful not to slide in the gravel. The footing was uncertain. Any misstep would send him careening down the embankment, ending his celebration before it began.

He steadied himself before moving forward but stopped short when he saw a flash of movement from the corner of his eye. He turned and focused his attention on the cliffs that topped the ravine's east wall. There was nothing, until–

Something black bobbed from behind a boulder then disappeared. Then, a moment later, a dark, winged figure appeared from behind a rock. The figure waved a hand and three more of his kind appeared from hiding. They were moving along a path parallel to Taylor's, ready to swoop down on the group when the time was right.

Wesley swallowed hard.

He wasn't the only one chasing Taylor.

And the monkeys were closer.

"Taylor!" He screamed so loudly this time that her name felt like a razor blade traveling the length of his throat.

She didn't turn.

Wesley hopped down the path. Gravel gave way beneath his feet like tiny rock slides. He didn't have time to be careful. Not if he was going to catch up with–

His foot slipped. He grabbed onto a twisted tree root protruding from the ravine's wall. He steadied himself then looked down at them again.

The monkeys were moving in on Tay and his friends. Wes used his free hand to cup his mouth, hoping it would help his voice carry so he wouldn't go unheard again. Instead, the ground gave way beneath his feet before he could call her name, and his weight pulled the dead tree root from the earth.

Wesley began to fall.

❖ ❖ ❖

The Lion stopped to drink from the stream, lapping up water with a fat tongue. Taylor thought it wise to do the same. The stream was the first water they'd seen since leaving camp, and the road ahead looked rocky. Who knew how long it might be before they saw water again?

After their drink, the Tin Man noticed Taylor was looking back once more.

"What is it?" he asked.

"Nothing," she said. "I just... I thought I heard something."

"Ah," the Tin Man said. "The wind can play tricks on you in a valley like this. I've seen it many times."

Taylor thought her eyes must have been in on the joke, too. She was sure she'd seen something on the cliffs above but saw there was nothing when she turned to look again.

She knelt for another drink. As soon as her attention shifted, the monkey she'd nearly spotted came out of hiding and took flight.

The Lion pulled away from the creek, his mane wet and dripping. He looked up just in time to see the monkey sailing toward them with its wings spread.

"Look out!"

The monkey swooped down and passed over the companions. It arced toward Taylor, but she dropped to her knees and fell just out of reach.

The companions scattered as more monkeys seemed to appear from nowhere. They came out of the brush. They jumped down from the cliffs above. They dropped from the sky. Tay thought she saw one of the winged demons spring out of the creek they'd been drinking from.

The others ran for cover, but Taylor quickly collected herself and held her ground.

She'd made it.

This was exactly where she was supposed to be.

In the book, Dorothy was captured by the monkeys. Taylor would let them take her, too. Just as the story demanded.

"R-r-run!" the Lion roared. *"What are you doing?!"* He galloped forward and tried to nudge her along with his nose. Tay pulled away.

"They're going to take us," she explained. "You and me. I know it's hard for you, but don't be scared."

"W-what are you t-talking about?! Go!"

One of the monkeys dropped beside them and bared his teeth in an ugly snarl. The Lion cowered, but Taylor didn't look.

"You're a lot braver than you think. You'll see."

◆ ◆ ◆

Battered and bloodied, Wesley arrived just in time to see one of the winged monkeys duck beneath the Tin Man's hammer. Momentum carried the hammer forward, and it caught the Scarecrow's chest and sent him flying.

"Taylor!"

Wesley had slid and somersaulted most of his way into the ravine, only stopping when his body crashed to a stop on a boulder near the bottom. His hands were scraped. Tree limbs and thorny bushes had opened jagged cuts on his arms and face.

Something in his leg had popped in the fall. And yet, somehow he'd made it – if not in time to warn them, in time to help.

Only he couldn't get Taylor's attention.

What is she doing?! he thought. *She's just standing there!*

He ran toward her and was just seconds away when a monkey dropped between them. The beast seemed to smile at Wesley before turning to grab his friend.

"No!" Wesley launched himself forward, sliding through the dirt and latching onto the monkey's leg. The creature screeched. With Wes dragging behind him, the monkey skidded across the ground, its giant wings batting the air to no avail. For a moment, it looked like Wesley's weight was enough to anchor the monkey down. But then, the monster looked back at Wesley with annoyance and promptly kicked at the boy's face. His grip loosened, and the monkey broke free.

"No!" Wesley screamed. *"No!"*

Wes leapt to his feet and charged after the monkey as it took flight with Taylor in its iron grip. He reached out again, diving forward, but this time all he got was a face full of dirt and hands full of air.

"No! Tay! Tay!"

He stumbled to his feet and sprinted after them. They were already thirty feet above him and rising fast.

No! Wesley thought. *No! No! No!*

Wes dodged everything in his path. He circled the Tin Man who was screaming at the monkeys, still fighting them off with his maker's hammer. He darted past the Cowardly Lion who was batting at two of the screeching monkeys and hiding behind a pathetic roar. He even ignored the Scarecrow as three monkeys held him down while another pulled the straw from his body.

None of that mattered. Wes couldn't help them. Their destiny had been written more than a century before. But Taylor's...

He raced after her.

She was sixty feet above him. Even farther out.

Please! he thought.

Eighty feet.

Please! Tay!

One hundred.

Turn! Look! One time! I'm here!

But she never did. Taylor never saw just how close he'd come to saving her – or that he'd even come at all.

Wesley watched her until she and her captor were nothing more than a pinprick of black in the sky. Soon after that, they were gone for good.

He fell to his knees and stared up at the empty sky while completely oblivious to everything that had happened around him: the Lion had been captured; the Scarecrow was left for dead; the Tin Man had been dropped onto jagged rocks meant to be his death. Wesley stayed there, oblivious to everything but her. He didn't even know he was sobbing until the end.

CHAPTER 20

DOUGLAS WATCHED UNTIL the crystal's pink smoke disappeared and took the image of Wesley and the others with it.

"Yes!" the Witch screamed. "See? What did I tell you?"

Douglas turned to Bones who was standing with his arms crossed. "Take Randy," he ordered. "Go out on the balcony to greet her."

"What?" Randy whined. "Why me?"

"She'll need to see a friendly face."

"But we *aren't* friends. She hates me!"

Douglas put a hand on Randy's shoulder. "You're all she's got, son. And she needs someone. Think how scared she must be right now." Randy looked down at the ground, but Douglas raised his chin. "If she hates you it's just because she doesn't know you yet." He turned Randy toward the door and gave him a little shove. "Now go."

Randy saw Bones waiting in the doorway and let the dark character lead him out of the room. He had so many questions running through his mind as they climbed the stairs in silence. How could his dad leave him alone with Bones like this again? What was so important about this book his dad was willing to kill for it? And who was his dad? Who was he *really*? This wasn't the same man who'd taught him to ride his bike, was it? He wasn't the same man who had pulled his baby teeth and built a tree house and camped under the stars with Randy. It couldn't be. Could it?

They were important questions. But right now they all took a backseat to the most pressing of all: what the heck was he going to say when Taylor got there?

◆ ◆ ◆

Wesley found the Scarecrow first. Most of the straw had been pulled from his body and tossed to the ground. Wes scrambled to collect it before it blew away then began stuffing the Scarecrow's clothes as best he could. Moments later, the Scarecrow sat up, the same old smile stitched into his face.

"What happened?" he asked.

Even without a brain, Wesley knew just a quick look around would give the Scarecrow his answer. He didn't have the heart to tell him himself.

Wes and the Scarecrow walked through the ravine together. Eventually, they heard the Tin Man's painful moans coming from a rocky area on the ravine's embankment. Wesley scaled the jagged boulders and helped the metal man to his feet.

"Thank you. I was beginning to think all of you'd been captured and I would be trapped alone like before." He looked about. "Where's Miss Taylor?"

The Scarecrow answered for Wesley. "The monkeys took her. The Lion, too."

Wesley started down the gravel path.

"Where are you going?"

"What's it look like? I'm going to save them."

Wesley's friends shared a nervous look.

"Wesley," the Scarecrow began, "I've grown to like Taylor a great deal. I want to save her too, but there's no way the three of us can kill the Witch alone."

"He's right," the Tin Man said. "Maybe everyone's right. Maybe we should just go back. We've lost two friends, and we haven't even made it to the gate."

Wesley stared into the distance. It did feel like a fool's errand. But Taylor wouldn't give up on him. He wasn't about to turn his back on her. Not again. He stood in silence for a long moment before finally speaking up.

"You're right," Wesley said. His voice was so low that it was barely audible.

"What do you mean?" the Scarecrow asked. "*Who's* right?"

"We'll go back." Wesley began to search for the trail that would lead them out of the ravine. He was carrying himself with a new air of confidence that neither the Scarecrow nor the Tin Man seemed to understand. "There's no way we can take the Witch's castle alone."

◆ ◆ ◆

Randy watched the winged monkey approach with Taylor. Its wings batted the air as it swooped down and dropped her onto the balcony beside him before flying away.

Taylor came to her feet and quickly checked her surroundings.

“Randy?” Taylor asked.

“Are you okay? They didn't hurt you, did they?”

“Hurt me? Randy? *What are you doing here?*”

“Me? I thought you went back home?”

“It's a long story. We came back to fix things.”

“You mean Bates is here, too?”

She couldn't tell if the concern in Randy's voice was real.

“What's going on, Randy?”

“My dad sent me.”

“Your dad?”

“Tay, there isn't time.”

He stepped toward her, but Taylor backed away.

“Don't call me that!” she said angrily.

“Okay,” he said. “Just calm down.”

“No! Why is your dad in Oz?”

“I don't know. Okay? This whole thing is about some book in the library. He says The Librarian promised it to him. Something like that. I don't know.” Randy was getting flustered. This wasn't how their conversation was supposed to go. “It doesn't matter. He's going to take you back with us. That's why he sent the monkeys."

"The Witch sent them, Randy."

"No she didn't! My dad did. Okay? He's going to help you get back, you just... you have to be nice about it."

"Yeah," Taylor smirked. "*That's* gonna happen."

"I'm serious, Taylor. Don't make him mad. My dad... he's different here. He's done things. Seriously, there's something... *off* about him."

That got Taylor's attention. Off. That's just how her father had acted.

"Randy, what's wrong?"

"Nothing!" Randy exclaimed.

He stuck out his chest and threw on a cocky grin. It was the same tough guy persona he hid behind in school, but Taylor could finally see through it. She looked at him sideways, and he melted beneath her stare. His shoulders slumped. His smile vanished. Finally giving in, he looked over at Bones before leaning in to whisper something in Taylor's ear.

"I'm scared, Taylor. I'm really scared."

◆ ◆ ◆

The Librarian was just about to give up when the lock clicked and his cell door creaked open. He slinked through the door then quickly left the room, bending his spectacles back into shape as he went.

CHAPTER 21

THE WITCH WAS through taking chances. By sundown, every guard in her kingdom was standing outside the castle gate. Wesley guessed there were fifty men waiting when he and the Tin Man made their approach.

One of the guards was wearing a metal helmet with a purple plume. He spotted the strangers, pointing in their direction as he stepped forward.

"You there! You! Don't make another move!"

Wesley and the Tin Man did as they were told.

The guard with the plume turned to the men behind him. "What do we do?"

"We're supposed to kill anyone we see," someone reminded.

"But it's just a boy? He's harmless."

"That other one doesn't look harmless to me." He gestured toward the Tin Woodsman with his spear. The lead guard with the plume nodded in agreement then turned his attention to Wesley and the Tin Man once more.

"Hurry," he said. "Turn and go! Before something bad happens to you!"

Wesley cleared his throat. "We'll go," he hollered. "We aren't here to fight. But the Witch is holding our friends prisoner. Convince her to let them go, and no one will get hurt here today."

The guards looked around at one another. Some snickered. Others snorted. Then the rest erupted in a chorus of belly laughs that could be heard for miles. Wesley flinched. He knew this would be their reaction but wasn't prepared for how small and insignificant it would make him feel.

One of the guards was doubled over with laughter. "Oh, child! We needed a good laugh. Thank you! Now, go on. Run back to your parents before you've worn out your welcome."

"I'm sorry," Wesley said. "We aren't going anywhere."

The guard giggled a moment longer, but the amusement disappeared from his face when he saw Wesley was serious.

"Don't be a fool, boy! If you don't leave, I'll send my men to get you, and you'll wish you had!"

Wesley shifted his weight. The Tin Man stood his ground.

The guard in the plume shook his head in frustration. He waved one of his men forward. The guard who'd seen Douglas shoot his crooked-nosed friend stepped out of the crowd.

"Me?" he asked tentatively.

"Yes," the guard said. "Go and get them."

"But sir, something's not right about this boy. Don't you agree? What if he's carrying one of those noisemakers like the man before? He'll kill us all."

The guard in the purple plume didn't like the sound of that.

"Tell me, boy. Are you carrying one of those noisy wands?"

"Noisy wands," Wesley smirked. "No."

"You have no weapons at all, then?"

"I didn't say that." Wesley looked up at the Tin Man. "Do your thing, Nick."

The Tin Man nodded then balled his fist and began to pound on his chest. The hollow thud echoed through the countryside. Instinctively, the guards moved into a defensive position: shields up with spears ready. But when nothing happened, they all began to laugh again.

"Oh, child! Your friend can beat on his chest all he likes. That isn't going to–"

The guard stopped short. There was a rustle of movement coming up the stone staircase. The others heard it, too. They looked their surroundings over once more, this time with worry in their eyes. A few pulled swords from their sheaths, just in case.

The lead guard looked out at Wesley, squinting his eyes to see if there was something he'd missed. His eyes widened.

"Battle positions!"

The villagers came up the staircase in a wave, all of them, every friend Taylor and Wes had made in their journey, all of them screaming as they charged the castle gate.

◆ ◆ ◆

Bones led Randy and Taylor from the castle balcony and into the Witch's chambers. They passed three nervous guards on their way. All three were rushing along; each was armed with a bow and had a quiver filled with arrows strapped across his back.

The Witch was screeching orders at two additional guards when Randy and Taylor entered the room. When she was done, both men hurried away.

Taylor looked over at Randy. "Is this normal?"

He shook his head. "What's happening, dad?"

Douglas turned away from the window to answer, but the Witch beat him to it.

"We're under siege!" she hissed. *"What does it look like?"*

Randy stepped to the window and looked out.

A battle was brewing on the grounds below. The Tin Man was leading a ragged group of peasants in an attack on the castle. The men engaged the castle guards while a mob of women and children charged toward the gate.

Randy turned to wave Taylor over, but she ignored him.

Something else had caught her eye.

Amidst the madness, a skinny maid in a patchwork dress was scrubbing the Witch's floor with a large brush. She was on her knees and only stopped swabbing the tiled stone occasionally to dip her brush in the bucket of soapy water beside her.

"We need to leave," Douglas explained.

"Retreat?" the Witch sneered. "I think not! I fought back the Great and Powerful Oz. Surely I can fend off a few starving peasants."

"The monkeys fought the Wizard back. Not you."

The Witch measured him with her one good eye. "Is this what you were talking about? This is written in your book that governs my world?"

"No." Douglas glanced out the window again. "This is something else."

◆ ◆ ◆

The Librarian hid behind a pillar when he heard the jangle of armor coming his way. He watched from hiding as a squad of castle guards rushed by. When they were gone, he started down the corridor again.

He'd found his staff and satchel in a small armory just outside his cell and had set off to find Douglas when something happened that sent a wave of nervous energy surging through the castle.

At first, The Librarian assumed they had been alerted to his escape, but he quickly realized they had more pressing concerns. Guards outside were yelling for the drawbridge to be raised. He heard the metallic clang of swords striking swords. And while he wasn't sure, he thought he heard the excited screams of children. It sounded like the castle was under attack – although that made little sense to him. He'd read *The Wonderful Wizard of Oz* more times than he could count. Only Oz the Great had ever dared to storm the Witch's castle, and he'd failed so miserably that no one had tried again.

But when The Librarian found a window, he saw that the people in Oz were indeed revolting against the Witch. He couldn't believe it! He stood and watched the action unfold until he saw two arrows cut through the air toward the villagers below. He looked up. There were now three archers in the watchtower, each ready to rain arrows down on those storming the castle.

The old man turned from the window and started quickly down the corridor again. He didn't know what was happening, but he knew he was going to help.

❖ ❖ ❖

Wesley saw one of the castle guards throw the Scarecrow through the air like a rag doll and hurried over to help him up.

"You okay?"

The Scarecrow nodded then threw up one of his floppy arms and pointed toward the castle's wooden drawbridge. "Look," he cried. "They're closing the gate!"

The battle was unfolding all around them. The Tin Man fought three guards at a time. The villagers used clubs and sticks and tools that weren't meant for fighting but made good weapons all the same. A few women had snuck past everyone and were helping their children climb through windows into the castle.

"Let's go!" Wesley yelled.

Together they ran for the castle's entry as a pair of guards worked tirelessly to raise the gate. They dodged swinging swords. They ducked beneath darting spears. Once, Wesley dropped to his knees as a pair of guards tried to grab him. Instead, they collided with each other and fell to the ground in a daze.

They were halfway there when the Scarecrow saw movement in one of the towers above them. "Look out!" he screamed.

Wesley stopped dead in his tracks, looking back at his friend. He couldn't read a thing in the Scarecrow's button eyes and instead followed his blank stare up to the watchtower where he caught sight of an archer just as he let his arrow fly.

The Scarecrow leapt forward. He tackled Wesley to the ground, but the arrow pierced the Scarecrow's back. He was on top of Wesley when the others came, arrows that made their home in the Scarecrow's leg, shoulder, and throat.

◆ ◆ ◆

The Witch took the pistol and held it out for Douglas. "Here," she said nervously. "Teach me this magic as you promised."

"That's not how it works," he explained. "You can't–"

"Then you stop them!"

Douglas drew a deep breath then gently touched the Witch on her hand. Her skin was cool beneath his fingers.

"One gun won't be enough. You have to take us away from here. We may lose this battle, but that doesn't mean we have to lose the war."

"But... I'm the ruler of Oz. *They* should cower before *me*."

"They will. I promise. But first–"

"I must help you."

"We'll help each other," Douglas said. "Just like we discussed. You get me back to the Tin Man's cabin, I'll do the rest."

"But the Tin Man lives in Munchkin Country!"

"Can't you fly us out of here on your broom?"

"My broom?" Her reaction was one of utter confusion.

"Yes. Don't you–"

Douglas heard snickering from the corner and looked over to the spot where his son was standing with Taylor.

"What?" he asked snidely.

"She doesn't have a broom," Taylor explained. "That's from the movie, not the book." She looked at Randy. "Guess he reads about as much as you do, huh?"

"Don't," Randy whispered.

"Maybe she can take us home on her umbrella," Taylor suggested.

The Witch flinched when she heard something crash in a nearby room. Some of the villagers had made it inside.

"Think," Douglas said. "Is there another way out?"

"There is," she said grimly. "But we don't need it. I have a spell that will do what you ask."

◆ ◆ ◆

Wesley dragged the Scarecrow's limp body through the dirt and toward a boulder that was sitting just a few feet away. Once hidden, he frantically began to check the Scarecrow for wounds.

"Oh my god! I'm so sorry! I should have seen!"

He wasn't moving. Wesley rolled him onto his back. Three arrows had pierced his body, but Wesley couldn't find any blood.

"Please wake up! Please—"

The Scarecrow popped up into a sitting position. Wesley fell back, startled by the happy expression that was still stitched onto the Scarecrow's face.

"Are... are you okay?"

"I think so." The Scarecrow patted his body down. "Everything seems to be in the right place." He began to pull the arrows from his body one at a time. They came out with ease. "I don't think weapons like this can hurt me."

Wesley flashed a toothy grin. "I bet you're scared to death of fire, though, huh?"

"I am," he answered happily. "How did you know that?"

"Call it a lucky guess."

Wesley poked his head out to check their path. The drawbridge was closing. In a few moments, their access to the castle would be gone.

"Is it clear?"

An arrow raced past. Wesley ducked for cover. All three archers had their arrows trained on the path leading into the castle.

"We're pinned down! We're not gonna make it!"

◆ ◆ ◆

The Witch had everything she needed scattered across the table in front of her: the severed foot of a chicken, an oversized egg, several rocks that looked like glass, and the carcass of a dead rabbit.

The Witch closed her eye and sighed. "I can't concentrate with you making all that noise, girl!"

Startled, the maid looked up from her work. Douglas looked down at her. The poor girl was trembling. "Why don't you find someplace safe to hide. Okay?" The young woman bowed her head then hurried out the door.

Once she was gone, Douglas shifted his attention back to the Witch. She'd just cracked the egg and was pouring its bloody yolk over the rocks on the table. When finished, the Witch tossed the eggshell aside and began stirring the rocks with the chicken foot. It was a strange display. Everyone was watching with morbid fascination. Everyone but Tay. Her eyes were now fixed on the maid's bucket of water sitting just a few feet away.

◆ ◆ ◆

The Librarian crept up the stairwell and into the castle's watchtower. All three archers had their backs to him, their eyes on the revolt happening below when the old man tripped over a discarded helmet and sent it bouncing loudly down the stairs.

The Witch's men turned. "Get him!"

His advantage gone, The Librarian cracked the first archer with his staff. The blow doubled him over. When he fell, his bow sent its arrow into the chest of the man beside him.

But the third archer didn't go down so easily. He charged forward and tackled The Librarian. The old man screamed out as new pain lit up the wound in his shoulder.

As if irritated by The Librarian's cry, the archer wrapped both hands around his throat and choked off any others before they came. He put his weight behind his grip and began to squeeze, watching with glee as the old man's eyes bulged and his face turned red.

The Librarian struggled to break free but couldn't. His vision blurred. His head felt light. Finally, in an act of desperation, he raised his knees into the archer's groin and broke free of the guard's grip.

The old man gasped for air. He reached for his staff, but the archer pulled him off his feet before he could grab it. He swung The Librarian through the air and pinned him to the ledge that looked down on the grounds below.

He leaned on The Librarian, hoping his size would force the old man over the side. The Librarian grabbed the stone ledge for support but the top bricks began to move beneath his weight. He tried to knee the archer away, but the guard was ready this time and evaded the pathetic attack with ease.

The old man looked back over his shoulder. More than a hundred feet above the ground, any fall would be fatal. The archer leaned on him. The Librarian's feet came off the ground as his body teetered over the ledge.

But then the old man's attention fell on the arrows in the quiver strapped to the archer's back. He reached out. His fingers grazed one of the arrows, but the guard pushed on him again and it fell out of reach.

The Librarian could feel the bricks giving way beneath him. Desperate, he lunged forward. This time he got what he was after. He pulled an arrow from the quiver and jammed its arrowhead into his attacker's chest.

The archer released The Librarian and backed away. He yanked on the arrow that was jutting from his chest, but it wouldn't budge.

Suddenly enraged, the archer charged toward The Librarian one final time, hoping to take the old man with him in his final moments of life. Instead,

The Librarian ducked, and the archer fell over the ledge to the ground below.

❖ ❖ ❖

Wesley heard the archer scream as he fell from the watchtower. He looked up, watching the man claw helplessly at the air in his descent. Wes took his eyes away when the guard crashed onto the rocks below.

"Did he jump?" the Scarecrow asked.

"I doubt it."

Wesley shifted his gaze back to the watchtower. His eyes widened with surprise when he caught a quick glimpse of The Librarian just seconds before the old man disappeared from view.

"C'mon!"

Wesley waved the Scarecrow forward, and they ran for the castle gate. They arrived just in time to climb onto the bridge before it was raised completely out of reach. But Wesley was beginning to feel like it was more than luck. He couldn't shake the idea something had been helping them all along. More and more he felt this was the way it was supposed to be. For now, Wes pushed the thought from his mind as he and the Scarecrow sprinted down the raised bridge and into the Witch's castle.

◆ ◆ ◆

The Witch chanted something beneath her breath and the rocks on the table began to glow. Strangely, Douglas saw that the Witch's body had become slightly translucent. It was barely noticeable at first, but the brighter the rocks grew, the more ghostlike the Witch's appearance became.

"Dad?"

Douglas looked over at Randy. Randy had both hands up in front of him and was looking at them with alarm. Like the Witch, he was beginning to fade. Douglas looked down at himself. He could see the castle's stone floor through his feet.

He took Randy's hand, ready to hold it until they reappeared in the meadow outside the Tin Man's cabin. Neither noticed that Taylor was now holding the bucket of water the maid had left behind.

◆ ◆ ◆

Wesley and the Scarecrow came into the castle's foyer just as The Librarian came down the steps.

"*Master Wesley?* What are you *doing here?*"

The boy looked up at the old man. When he answered he didn't explain that he'd come to save Oz or that he was trying to bring The Librarian his amulet or that he was there to kill the Wicked Witch. Instead, all he said was: "I'm here to save Tay."

Wesley started down the long corridor in front of him. He looked into each of the rooms he passed, only moving on when he saw Taylor wasn't there. The Librarian joined the Scarecrow, both ready to help Wesley in his search.

The castle was alive with activity, but most of the guards paid Wesley and his friends little mind. They were in full retreat. The villagers had won.

Eventually, Wesley came into an empty dining room with a spiral staircase in the corner. Its steps extended in both directions. Wesley weighed the choices before him then heard Douglas Stanford screaming from atop the staircase.

He began to climb.

◆ ◆ ◆

"NO!" Douglas yelled. *"What are you doing?!"*

Douglas stepped toward Taylor, but it was too late.

The Witch broke from her trance and turned just in time to see Taylor heave the bucket forward. The Witch gasped. She watched helplessly as the water flew toward her then wailed in pain as it washed over her body.

Her body solidified to its normal state the moment the water struck. Then, just as quickly, her green skin began to bubble and melt, running down her face like the wax on a burning candle. Her ears slid down her cheeks. The bottom of her jaw fell, stretching the skin around her mouth so it was now resting on her chest. She began to shrink as the water ate away her legs.

"What have you done?!" the Witch shrieked.

Everyone was transfixed as they watched the Witch die; Taylor knew this was her only chance for escape.

But Taylor noticed that the *castle around her* was now beginning to fade. *It* was becoming the ghost as their bodies came back into focus. There was grass at her feet. She could see trees through the castle walls as they began to disappear. Her surroundings were morphing into the meadow outside the Tin Man's cabin. It felt as if she were standing in both places at once. In a moment, the castle would be gone and she'd be on the other side of Oz with Douglas, Randy, and Bones.

Tay darted toward the staircase but knew she wasn't going to make it when she saw Wesley running up the stairs toward her. That's what she *wanted* to see: Wesley storming the castle to save her. But Taylor was sure he wasn't there. She convinced herself he was nothing more than a mirage: her wishful thinking mingled with the magic that was taking them away.

She stopped and let the castle around her vanish.

The Witch's spell had worked.

◆ ◆ ◆

Wesley hurried up the steps and rounded the corner into the Witch's throne room. He looked about. Douglas was gone. So was anyone who'd been with him.

Wesley looked down at the Wicked Witch and cringed.

"Help me, please!"

Even if he wanted to, there was nothing Wesley could do. Most of the Witch had melted away into a puddle of green sludge on the floor. All that remained was the upper part of her torso. Most of the skin on her face was gone. She was little more than a pile of bones held together by a web of grisly pink muscles and tendons.

"I've been... terribly wicked in my day... but I never thought... a little girl... would... ever..." With that, she was gone, nothing left behind but her clothes floating in the green goo.

"I'm sorry," The Librarian said softly. "I believe we've missed her."

Wes shook his head and tried to smile. "Don't be," he said. He looked up at the old man, and for a brief moment, The Librarian wasn't looking down at the boy he'd met just a few days before. Instead, he saw the honorable man Wesley Bates would one day become.

"Taylor did it," he said proudly. "She really did."

CHAPTER 22

TAYLOR TRIED TO run, but Douglas grabbed her before she could get too far. "You're a little brat, you know that?"

They were in the meadow outside the Tin Man's cabin.

"Do you know what you've done?" Douglas grabbed Taylor by her shoulders. When she didn't answer, it infuriated Douglas so much that he gave her a violent shake. "What? No smart-mouth jokes to tell? I should just leave you behind. We'll see how funny you are then!"

"Dad?"

Taylor whimpered as he jerked her back and forth.

"Dad!"

Douglas finally looked away and saw his son was frightened. He turned to glare at Taylor a little longer then shook her one last time before letting go.

"You love this girl as much as I do, huh?"

Everyone turned to see who belonged to the voice that was coming from inside the cabin. Taylor looked too, but her eyes had narrowed to angry slits. She had recognized the voice immediately.

Hope strutted through the cabin's door and into the meadow. "I was hoping you would have learned to be a bit more respectful while out in the world on your own, Taylor."

"What are you doing here? Where's Wesley?"

"Poor kid went looking for you."

Taylor stormed past her into the cabin. Hope waited patiently for Taylor to reappear once she'd seen no one was waiting inside.

"I told him you weren't worth it," Hope smirked.

"What did you do to him?"

"I tried to stop him. But he was just so angry that you lied."

"I didn't lie to him," Taylor snapped.

"Yeah, you did. And just think, that's probably the last thing he's gonna remember about you. Isn't that sweet?"

Taylor gritted her teeth and lunged toward Hope.

"Whoa!" Hope backpedaled away until Bones stepped in and stopped Tay with ease. She kept reaching for Hope, though, kicking and screaming as the hooded man held her back.

"You freakin' witch! You were lying to us the whole time! You're gonna lecture me! I swear, if something happens to him..."

"You'll what?" Hope sneered.

Taylor let her cold stare linger on Hope before looking away when her emotions finally got the best of her. Her fury was real, but as it often does, anger gave way to the heartbreak and desperation she was now feeling. Tears were on their way.

Hope stepped toward Douglas. "You sure you want to take her with us?"

"Tell me you've got good news," he said.

Douglas watched as Hope unfastened the top two buttons on her blouse to reveal Wesley's amulet hanging around her neck.

"Look at that," he said. "We match." He pushed his shirt collar aside to show Hope that he had an amulet hanging around his neck, too. It was similar to hers, only its markings were different.

Douglas kissed her gently on the lips then took the amulet from around his neck and fell to one knee. "Let's get out of here. What do you say?"

Everyone watched as Douglas stepped toward the Tin Man's cabin with the amulet raised in one hand. It began to glow as he moved it closer to the shack's wall. When the amulet's thin edge touched the cabin, it pushed through the wood and purple light began to shine through from the other side. The amulet left a thin line of pink light in its wake as Douglas traced the cabin's entry with the powerful relic. When he was finished, the magical glow of a new portal began to fill the empty doorway.

Taylor let her gaze drift into the meadow. The grass was still dead, the flowers wilted. The trees in the distance were bare. The yellow brick road was gone. Everything looked exactly as it had when they'd returned. Nothing had changed. Killing the Witch hadn't worked. They'd gone through all this for nothing. Her life in Astoria would be the same nightmare she'd left behind – only now, Wesley would be gone too.

Her eyes welled with tears. She wanted to run off. Maybe this time she could get away. Maybe this time they'd let her. She had no idea where she would go – only that she wanted to be all alone when she got there.

But then, her gaze locked on something in the distance.

There was a single pink rose growing in the spot where she and her mother had met their demise in Taylor's nightmare, one stroke of color on an otherwise drab canvas.

The cabin's doorway had become nothing but a pool of shimmering light. Douglas motioned everyone through. When Taylor didn't move, Bones took her by the hand and yanked her along with him. Tears streamed down her face. She had no idea what Douglas would eventually do with her. The truth was, she didn't care. Instead, she looked back into the meadow as Bones pulled her along, praying her tears hadn't clouded her vision and filled her with false hope.

She blinked hard and looked once more toward the spot where her mother had fallen. Only now there wasn't a single flower growing in the meadow like she thought...

There were three.

CHAPTER 23

WESLEY AND THE Librarian found the Scarecrow waiting for them at the bottom of the castle staircase. "The Tin Man's gone to find the Lion," he said.

"Good," Wesley answered.

"The villagers want to know what we should do with the captured guards."

"Let them go. They were slaves, too. They weren't fighting us because they wanted to. The Witch would have killed them if they didn't follow her orders."

The Scarecrow glanced up the stairwell, confused when he saw that The Librarian was the only one who had followed Wesley down.

"Where's Miss Taylor?"

Wesley frowned and shook his head.

"Oh..."

The Scarecrow turned, shoulders slumped as he padded away.

"We'll get her back," The Librarian promised. Wesley nodded then started to walk away. The old man followed. "Something told me the two of you would return. I'm told it's hard for kids to come just once. I take it you came back once you saw you'd made changes to the story?"

Wesley looked down at his feet. "We wanted to fix it – not that we did much good."

"I think you did better than you know."

"I don't see how."

They started across the drawbridge. Outside, many of the villagers who'd helped him were now making friends with the guards they'd fought just moments before.

Nell elbowed her father when she saw Wesley standing on the bridge outside the castle gate. When he saw Wes covered in mud and cuts and bruises, a proud smile crept onto the man's face. He began to clap. The applause drew peculiar looks from those around him until they saw Wesley, too. A moment later, everyone else joined in to applaud everything Wesley had done.

Embarrassed, Wesley gave an appreciative wave but looked away.

"See that?" The Librarian asked. "They understand. The Witch is dead. Her slaves are freed. Things aren't exactly where they need to be, but the story seems to be heading in the right direction." Wesley nodded, but he didn't seem convinced. "Did you bring the book I gave you?"

"Yeah," Wesley said.

"Give it to me, please."

Wesley took off his backpack then slid the large, leather-bound book from the pack's main pouch. The Librarian began to smile as he flipped through its pages.

"What is it?" Wesley asked.

"See for yourself."

Wesley moved to the old man's side and looked into the book. The words were swirling on the page. Wes watched with wonder as the letters melted away until they were nothing more than a black whirlpool of moving ink on the page.

"What's happening?"

"I told you," The Librarian said. "The story's begun to correct itself." He handed the book back to Wesley. "Tell me, how did you find Dorothy's companions? Did you have to search far-and-wide, or did events unfold in a way that you just happened upon them?"

Wesley took a moment to think. "We found the Tin Man first. We had a pretty good idea where to look for him. But then... well... I guess we got lucky."

"But it wasn't luck, Wesley!" The old man leaned on his staff for support. "Stories are living, breathing things. Like anything in nature, they can adapt. The *Oz* story wants to be fixed. It *needs* to be fixed. The story pushed you in the right direction, Wesley. I suspect things will shift in Oz again, and people will be much happier with the outcome this time."

Wesley looked up at the sky. The Tin Man had told them stories about the first shift in Oz. It didn't sound like something he wanted to experience for himself.

"Who knows?" The Librarian said. "Maybe the real world has a way of correcting itself, too. If you weren't here to help I'm not sure how I would have made it back myself. Tell me, where is the bookmark that was in your book?"

Wesley's heart sank. The Librarian looked like he'd aged a decade in the days since Wesley met him, but his demeanor was upbeat and hopeful. The old man was convinced they'd only suffered a minor setback, but Wesley knew the truth. He didn't know what The Librarian and Douglas Stanford were fighting over, but he knew The Librarian had lost. The portal between worlds could only be opened if you had the key. Wesley didn't have the amulet. They were trapped in Oz. He was about to break the old man's heart.

Dang, he was getting good at that.

EPILOGUE

MORNING LIGHT FILTERED through a dirty window into Captain Hook's quarters. The pirate was seated at his desk with his chin propped on both hands. His bloodshot eyes were fixed on the small device on the desk in front of him.

Smee sat in the corner. His cap was pulled down over his eyes so his captain wouldn't see he was trying to sleep. It had been a long night. Smee was beginning to think even the brilliant Captain Hook wasn't smart enough to figure out how to use the "button" given to him by the strange man who claimed to be from the "real world."

Smee was just about to nod off when Hook slammed a fist down on his desk and bellowed out in anger. Smee blubbered awake. His hat fell to the floor as he jumped to his feet.

"W-what is it, capt'n?"

"What do you think, Smee? It's always the same. I just don't know why I didn't see it before!" Hook pushed back on his chair and rose to his feet. "That man I met was working for Peter Pan! I'm sure of it! This is just another one of his elaborate pranks. Oh, Peter. Bad form. Such bad form, even for you and your wretched Lost Boys! This is a new low!"

The pirate started toward the door.

"What are you fixin' to do, capt'n?"

The pirate used his hook to point at the black device sitting on his desk. "What I should have done from the start, Smee. I'm going to fetch my mallet and crack that button as if it were one of my clocks."

"But, capt'n! We don't know what it is! What if–"

"It's nothing, Smee. It's absolutely–"

All at once, a strange melody began to play from somewhere inside the room. Hook stopped in the doorway. He looked back toward his desk. The music was coming from *inside* the strange device. The "button" had lit up and was vibrating in a way that sent it dancing across the desktop in time with the peculiar tune.

"Capt'n?"

"Quiet, Smee!"

Hook crept toward his desk. Smee followed. When the music stopped, Hook did the same. Smee didn't, though. He plowed right into the pirate and nearly knocked him over.

"You fool, Smee!"

"I'm sorry, capt'n." Both men started slowly toward the desk again. "What happened? Did it die?"

"I don't–"

The music began to play once more. Both men jumped. This time, Hook quickly collected himself and reached for the device.

"Careful, capt'n."

Hook picked it up and studied it closely.

"What about those numbers?" Smee asked.

Hook ignored him. He'd seen the numbers, too. Ten of them across the item's glass face. But now there was a strange green light that had captured Hook's attention. He pressed it, and the music turned quiet again.

"What happened, capt'n? You break it?"

"No, you twit. The lights are still on. See?"

"I know, but–"

Hook slapped a hand across Smee's mouth.

"Did you hear that, Smee?"

Smee tried to answer but couldn't. It didn't matter. Hook was sure he'd heard someone call his name from *inside the device*. A fairy, perhaps.

He held it to his ear and listened.

"Captain?" It was a man's voice.

"Yes? This is Captain Hook. Who am I speaking with?"

Miles away, Douglas Stanford stood near the peak of a tall mountain that offered an incredible view of Neverland island. His companions were with him, too. Randy and Taylor were astonished at their new surroundings. Taylor could see the Indian Camp on a peninsula in the distance. Randy had his eyes fixed on Skull Rock and the Jolly Roger anchored nearby.

Douglas had a cell phone pressed to his ear as he spoke. "This is Douglas Stanford, Captain. We spoke several days ago. I gave you the device you're holding. Do you remember?"

"I do."

"That's good," Douglas said. "I'm here to help you, Captain. Just as we discussed. I know how devilish those Lost Boys can be, and they've been giving you too much trouble. It's hard to win a war when your opponent is always breaking the rules, isn't it?"

"It is. But you need me to help you with something first. Am I remembering this correctly? Something about a magical book hidden within a library?"

Douglas grinned. "Meet me near Hangman's Tree. We'll discuss everything when you arrive. For now, just understand that I'm building an army... and we desperately need a captain."

ALSO BY ERIC HOBBS

<u>The Librarian</u>

Little Boy Lost

Unhappily Ever After

A Pirate's Revenge

<u>Nightcrawler Tales</u>

88 Keys

Attack of the Bandage Man

<u>The Magic of Race Bailey</u>

ABOUT THE AUTHOR

Since his debut, Eric Hobbs has seen his work published by DC Comics, Dark Horse, and NBM. His debut graphic novel, *The Broadcast*, was nominated for the ALA's annual "Great Graphic Novels for Teens" list before being named "Graphic Novel of the Year" by influential website Ain't It Cool News. *The Librarian* is his first novel.

Made in the USA
Lexington, KY
13 September 2018